ICE BURN

DUMFRIES
19

A
LAKESHORE U
STORY

ICE BURN

LAKESHORE U

L A COTTON

Published by Delesty Books

Edited by Kate Newman
Proofread by Sisters Get Lit.erary Author Services
Cover designed by Lianne Cotton

LAKESHORE U

Bite the Ice
A Lakeshore U Prequel Story

Ice Burn
A Lakeshore U Story

Break the Ice
A Lakeshore U Story

CHAPTER 1

DAYNA

"Mom, Dad, it's me." I slipped into the hallway, stuffing the key into my pocket, bags hanging off my arm.

"Dayna, is that you?" Dad's gruff voice carried through the house, hitting me right in the heart. I inhaled deeply, letting the smell of familiarity fill my lungs.

I was home.

Home.

"A little help," I called, moving further into the hallway.

"I could have gotten those," Josh grumbled behind me, and I rolled my eyes, gripping the handles a little tighter. Of course, he could have gotten them. But there was no use in offering once he'd watched me struggle all the way from the car to the house.

"Judy, get in here. Dayna's home."

"Already? She wasn't due for another hour."

A huge smile cracked over my face. It was typical of Mom to question the truth. Hell, she'd question the truth if it turned up wearing an 'I'm the truth shirt' and swore to tell the whole truth and nothing but the truth with one hand placed firmly on the Bible.

"Just get in here already."

"Where should I put this?" Josh's voice pulled me from the emotion swelling in my chest, and I groaned, "By the stairs," when really, I wanted to tell him to stuff his one bag where the sun didn't shine.

"There she is, my Dayna Bug. Get in here and give your old man a hug."

"Dad," I shrieked, launching myself at him. "God, I've missed you." My arms slipped around his back, and he squeezed me so tight it hurt.

"Not as much as me, Bug, not as much as me."

"Is she here? Where is she?" Mom's voice sounded a little choked as she appeared in the hallway, peeling grass-stained gloves off her hands.

I peeked out from Dad's chest.

"Oh, thank the Lord, there you are." She wrapped

her arms around Dad and me, and the three of us stood there hugging the crap out of each other until someone behind me cleared their throat.

"Hi, I'm Josh."

Mom squeezed me tight once more before releasing me, but I had to shirk out of Dad's hold, beaming up at him before turning to my boyfriend. "Mom, Dad, this is Josh. Josh, my parents, Judy and Derek Benson."

Josh stuck his hand out and said, "So nice to finally meet you both."

I didn't miss his emphasis on the word 'finally.'

Dad thrust his hand against Josh's, and they shook hands for a little longer than seemed appropriate. When it reached cringe-worthy proportions, I stepped between the two of them.

"Uh, Dad, I think you can give Josh his hand back now," I laughed, trying to ease the tension that had descended, telling myself this was completely normal. He was the first boyfriend I'd ever brought home—my first boyfriend, period. Dad was bound to be a little overprotective.

"Come on, let's get you both settled." Mom started doing her thing. "I made brownies. Just how you like them, Bug."

Josh caught my eye and mouthed 'bug' at me, but I

shook my head. I wasn't going there, not now. Not when I was so overwhelmed to be home.

"Did you have a good journey?" Dad asked, pulling out a chair for me, leaving Josh to fend for himself.

"It was okay. I drove to Syracuse, and then Josh did the rest. Took us about eleven hours in total." My muscles ached, my ass was numb, and I wanted to sleep for a week, but that was to be expected, just like the frown crinkling his eyes.

"You drove all that way?"

"Yeah, I drove all that. It's not a big deal." My eyes widened, warning him not to make a fuss out of nothing.

"I told her we should have stopped over some-where," Josh added, and I shot him a glare over the table where he was now seated. We'd already had this argument; I wasn't about to have it again in front of my parents.

"I didn't want it to take any longer than necessary." I just wanted to get home. Because if I didn't do it, there was every chance I would have turned around and gone back.

So what if it had taken us eleven hours, and I'd driven most of the way? It was done now, and I didn't plan on doing it again any time soon.

"Well, we're just glad you're back, sweetheart. Now,

who wants tea?" Mom held up the pot, and I smiled. It was the one she saved for special occasions.

"Yes, please, Mrs. Benson."

"Call me Judy. For the love of my young skin, call me Judy, please."

I stifled a laugh, and Josh added, "Well, in that case, thanks, Judy."

She poured Josh tea and then worked her way around the other cups. Also, her best ones. The ones that only came out when we had important guests, like the time Dad's boss had come over for dinner.

I added cream and sugar, shooting Dad a look. It was his turn to stifle a laugh as he mouthed, "You know how she gets."

I did, and I loved her for it all the same.

"Now, I didn't know if you wanted to eat out tonight or stay in, so I haven't made dinner yet, but I can whip something up?" Mom took her seat, tucking stray brown curls behind her ears.

I opened my mouth to reply, but Josh beat me to it. "We're pretty beat, so we'll probably want an early night, right, babe?"

Well, all right then.

"I guess." I smiled through my teeth, adding, "But we can order in, Mom, no need to make a fuss. There's plenty of time."

A noise that could only be described as a whimper of joy tumbled out of her mouth. "I still can't believe you're home. For good. Isn't it just amazing, Derek? Our baby is home."

Dad patted her hand across the table.

"You'll be sick of me in no time," I said, my chest tightening.

Mom smiled, and I couldn't be certain, but it looked like she was mopping tears out of the corner of her eyes.

"No tears, remember? You promised."

"I'm too damn happy to cry," Dad chimed in. "And what about you, Josh? What are your plans for the summer?"

"I'm headed to Toledo on Wednesday, sir."

"So soon?" Mom's brows pinched as she glanced at me. I gave her a small shrug. When I'd told them I was bringing Josh home with me, it still hadn't been decided how long he would stay.

"Unfortunately, yes. I start my new job Monday, and I want to get settled. But hopefully, I'll be able to see more of you guys soon." He smiled, and Mom nodded with a smile of her own.

"A lawyer in the making, how exciting."

She liked him; I could tell. I smiled too, feeling relieved that at least one of them did because Dad, well, Dad looked like he was sizing Josh up from across the room.

I placed my hand over his and squeezed. "Hey, big guy, go easy on him," I whispered. "Josh is a good guy."

But I wasn't quiet enough, and Josh almost choked on a mouthful of his tea while Mom's eyes went wide. Jesus, this was going well.

"You don't need to worry about sleeping arrangements or anything. Josh has family friends he can stay with when he visits." They lived in the next town over, but it was close enough.

Doing the long-distance thing was going to suck, but it was only a ninety-minute drive, so hopefully, we'd still see each other plenty. I'd always planned on coming back after I graduated to complete an internship at The Erie Echo. I had dreamed of working for the prestigious newspaper since I was a starry-eyed girl with big dreams of becoming the next Lois Lane. And it just so happened their HQ was a stone's throw away from Dupont Beach. I hadn't planned on meeting Josh, but I knew better than most that life could throw you a curveball at any given moment.

"Worried? Who's worried?" Dad scoffed. "I already made up the guest room, which is down here, I'm afraid." He looked anything but regretful about that.

But it didn't faze Josh as he flashed my father a

charming smile. "Sounds good to me, Mr. B. I know how it is."

I stared at him, wondering what the hell had gotten into him when the back door flew open. "Is she home?" The voice wrapped around me like a warm blanket. "Dayna Bug, get over here and give me a hug."

Before I knew what I was doing, I was out of the chair and rushing into Carson's arms. "God, it's so good to see you," I whispered, letting him cocoon me.

I'd forgotten how good it felt to be enveloped in his six-three frame. How safe it made me feel. He didn't reply, just held on like he couldn't believe I was here, and I gobbled it up just as I did with every other hug he'd ever given me.

"I fucking missed you," he eventually murmured against my hair, low enough that the words were for me and me alone. I smiled. Okay, so maybe I grinned like a fool.

We'd stayed in touch over the years and seen each other enough at holidays and family events, but each time I had to say goodbye to him and return to my life in Boston.

This time there was no saying goodbye to him.

Carson Walsh.

My best friend in the whole world.

The guy who had mopped up more tears than I

cared to remember, not to mention all the tubs of Ben and Jerry's we'd eaten together.

Someone coughed, and I froze.

Crap.

Carson's face left my neck, and he looked over my shoulder just as Josh said, "Dayna?"

Double crap.

"Hey, man." Carson hugged me into his side and ruffled my hair in that annoying way an older brother might. "I'm Carson."

"Carson, right." Josh stood up and came around the table, his hand already extended in front of him. "I'm Josh, Dayna's boyfriend," he said stiffly.

The word seemed to puncture the air, but if Carson noticed, he didn't let on as he slid his hand into Josh's and smiled wide. "Nice to meet you."

If I had worried about the awkward handshake between Dad and Josh, it had nothing on this. Neither man seemed willing to let up, and after another couple of painful seconds, I clapped my hands and said, "Well then, now we're all introduced... Mom, how about those brownies?"

She leapt into action, fetching plates from the cabinet. Josh returned to the table, but not before clutching the back of his neck and regarding Carson for another second. And Carson, arm still firmly around my shoulder, led me to the table, pulled out my chair, and tucked me in as I sat.

"You add in the extra chips, Judy?" He went over to Mom and helped her divvy up the brownies onto the plates like it was the most natural thing in the world. I felt Josh's eyes on me, burning holes in the side of my head, but I couldn't meet his glare. It would have to wait until later—in private—when I'd have to explain why I had failed to mention Carson.

At least Carson played a better game than him because if he were surprised I'd shown up with a boyfriend in tow, he didn't act like it. Until he pulled up a stool beside Mom, opposite me, and his big knowing brown eyes met mine.

Crap, I knew that look. It was the same look he'd given me so many times before.

Explain yourself, Dayna Bug.

Yeah, this wasn't going to be awkward at all.

CHAPTER 2

DAYNA

"I'M GOING to grab a shower, if that's okay?" Josh whispered; his hand firmly rested on my knee. Perhaps a little tighter than usual.

But then, I had dropped Carson on him without any warning, so I'd give him his overly possessive grip this once. As soon as we had a private moment, I intended to tell him to drop his territorial macho bull-shit. I wasn't a prize to be won; besides, he already had me.

He had *nothing* to be worried about.

I smiled at him, "Sure. I'll show you where every-thing is."

"You sit, sweetie. I'll show Josh around." Mom rose

from the couch. "We still haven't gotten around to remodeling the small bathroom, and the shower is temperamental. I don't want you to end up scalded. Come on; I'll give you the grand tour."

Uncertainty glittered in Josh's eyes, a look that said he would have preferred to have me show him around. But not wanting to be impolite, he forced a smile and said, "Thanks, Judy."

Josh leaned in and gave me a quick peck on the lips. I braced myself for the over-the-top PDA I expected to follow, but it didn't come. Nonetheless, I still blushed.

Almost twenty-two and blushing. Yeah, I was lame, but it was the first time I'd been kissed by a guy in front of my dad and Carson, and from the embarrassment weighing heavy on my chest, it was going to take a while to get used to.

"Mr. Ben— I mean, Derek, Carson, nice meeting you both. I'll see you later." Josh followed my mom out of the living room, and I sank back against the oversized cushions lining the couch.

No one spoke. Some documentary played on the television in the background, but we hadn't been watching it.

For the last hour, we'd talked about everything and anything. Everyone was just happy I was back and in one piece. Well, everyone except for Josh. I still wasn't sure how he felt about me moving home. But he knew my plans when we'd first started dating, so he'd had long enough to get used to the idea.

I looked over at my father in his armchair, his hands clasped in his lap. He gave me a tight-lipped smile. I tilted my head to one side, trying to figure out what he was thinking, when I caught the same expression on Carson's face.

"Okay, you two, what is it?" They both shot me a 'we don't know what you're talking about' look, and I groaned. "No, come on, out with it. Lay it on me. I'm a big girl."

Carson's seriousness slipped away for a second, and I used it to my advantage. "You." I jabbed my finger at him. "Out with it."

His hands flew up at his sides in surrender. "Oh no, I think this is a conversation for a father and his daughter, right, Derek?" My dad made an uncomfortable choking sound in his throat but still didn't say anything.

"Unbelievable," I mumbled. "Well, in that case, I'm going to wash the dishes. I'll let you two stew over whatever it is you want to say but are too chickenshit to do so." I arched my eyebrow at them and left the room.

I fully expected Carson to lay it on me, but he'd wait until the time was right, which usually meant out of earshot of my parents. That was just how we worked.

For as long as I could remember, he'd been the little voice over my shoulder, telling me when something wasn't such a good idea or reassuring me that everything would be okay. And he'd always been right.

Somewhere along the way, he'd become like a big brother to me. Sure, there had been a time when I'd crushed on him so hard that I couldn't look him in the eyes, but that was before. Now I loved him like I'd loved my brother.

Right on cue, I felt his presence behind me as I rinsed off the dishes in the soapy water. "I know you're there," I half laughed, sweeping the sponge over the plate.

"You always could sense me a mile away, Dayna Bug." He moved closer, leaning back against the counter next to me, folding his arms over his chest.

"You look good. Older." I shot him a playful look. "But good."

Broad shoulders and muscular arms that bulged out from underneath his black tee and gave way to a tapered waist and a firm stomach. I knew because I'd seen him enough times working out, mowing the lawn shirtless, or hanging out at the beach.

Carson was the epitome of good-looking with his mischievous smirk, sparkling green-blue eyes, and styled hair that was a shade of browny-blond most girls only prayed the salon could achieve. It was annoying, really. And don't get me started on the girls, the never-ending rotation of girls that had been present in my school days, vying for his attention. But he was a good person—the best kind.

He shook his head with laughter. "I'm almost twenty-six, Bug, hardly ancient. And I know I look good. I spend at least five minutes every morning telling myself that very thing in the mirror."

Snatching the towel off the hook, I snapped it in his direction. He ducked, laughing.

"You are so full of it."

Our laughter didn't last long enough, and then he asked the question I knew he was dying to, "You didn't tell me?"

The question was like a knife to my heart, and my hands sank further into the water. I'd known he would be disappointed.

For the last seven years, keeping something from Carson had been impossible. When two people went through what we had, there was no room for secrets. But this—Josh—was different.

"I..." My head craned up, meeting his heavy gaze. He deserved the truth. "I wanted one thing that was mine."

He just stared. He didn't speak, smile, or even frown. Carson just stared.

"Besides, it's not like you haven't been busy with your own life too, Cars." I deflected the limelight back on him. "How is Lakeshore U, by the way?"

He'd been busy with the Lakeshore U Lakers hockey team for the last couple of years. I'd been dating Josh for almost eight months. There just hadn't been a good time to drop it on him.

"Nice deflection, Bug." He smiled, and the temporary tension melted away. "It was good, busy. I'm glad to be home for the summer. I'm glad you're home."

Usually, at a moment like this, we would hug. It was kind of our thing, but I didn't move. I couldn't. So I blurted out, "He's a good guy, Cars."

"I'm sure he is. Just would have been nice to hear it from you and not your folks." His voice was flat, cool even, and I inhaled a quick breath. Carson's approval was important to me, and I didn't want any drama. I wanted my two favorite people to get along.

"Carson, come on." I shot him a sideways glare. *Give me a break*; I wanted to add.

"Does he make you happy?"

"Very." I didn't even have to think about it. Josh drove me a little insane and didn't always channel his inner gentleman, but he was a good guy. He'd been nothing but generous and kind and patient with me over the last eight months.

"Do you love him?"

He went there. Of course, he went there. It was something my brother Dalton would have said had he been around. Damn him.

"I—"

"I left Josh with towels and instructions on how not to flood the bathroom." Mom breezed into the kitchen, completely unaware of the awkwardness between Carson and me.

"Thanks, Mom."

She dropped a kiss on the side of my head and then went to Carson. "Gosh, it's just like old times seeing the two of you in here."

"Plenty more where that came from, Judy." Carson caught her around the waist and hugged her to him, making Mom giggle—full-on high-school crush giggle.

Lord, help me.

Not that I blamed her. Over the years, I watched more than one girl fall at Carson Walsh's annoyingly good-looking and charming feet.

When he released her, she had that dreamy doe-eyed look that had me rolling my eyes at her. "What?" she fake-gasped.

"Hussy," I grumbled, shooting her a 'you know what' look.

Mom glanced between us, and I was pretty sure her smile couldn't get any wider if she tried. "My heart's so full it could burst."

The playful moment from only seconds ago slipped away.

"My family is back right where they should be." She slung her arms wide, capturing us both. And I went willing because what else was there to do?

She was right; we were family.

And by God, if it didn't feel good to be back.

"Hey." I knocked again, poking my head around the door. "Can I come in?"

Josh smiled and patted the space beside him on the guest bed. "Are you sure your dad won't mind? He didn't seem to like the idea of me coming around a lot."

I slipped into Josh's arms, kicking my legs up in front of me. "Don't worry about Dad. He's just looking out for me. I told you this was new territory for me, Josh. I've never brought a guy home before."

We'd had this talk already when I'd invited him to come and stay before his job in Toledo started.

"And Carson, did he just slip your mind in that conversation?"

"Josh," I sighed. He was right, it didn't look good, but Carson belonged to a time in my life I still wasn't entirely comfortable sharing.

"Come on, Dayna, or is it Dayna Bug now? You kind of blindsided me."

Twisting in his arms, I tucked my legs to the side so that I was facing him. "Josh, you have nothing to worry about. Carson is a friend."

It was only a tiny lie, but I didn't want to alienate Josh any more than I already had. And truth be told, I didn't know how to explain what Carson and I shared.

It was... complicated.

"He looked more than just a friend to me."

"There's history there, yes, but not the way you're thinking." I hesitated, a heavy weight plunking in my chest. "He was my brother's best friend."

"Oh." Josh rubbed the back of his neck, his eyes looking anywhere but at me.

"Hey, hey." I slid a hand to his jaw, gripping gently. "I should have told you, but I knew you'd be weirded out by it. Carson is a friend, nothing more. I promise you have nothing to worry about."

Josh wound his arm around my waist and pulled me close, sealing his lips over mine. It was nice, comfortable. Kissing Josh was like riding the Ferris Wheel at the fairground. Smooth and steady. Pleasant. But it didn't get my heart racing.

He shifted, drawing me closer, his other hand gliding down my body. I snatched his wrist. "Josh, we can't. My parents are still awake."

He touched his head to mine, drawing in a ragged breath. "You can't keep doing this to me."

"Doing what?" I pulled away and frowned.

"You started it, *Bug*."

A strained laugh escaped my lips. "Please, no bug talk."

He shrugged his shoulders, but I could see the dejection in his eyes. "Too much, huh?"

"It's just a dumb nickname." I leaned in and kissed him again. "Give Carson a chance for me? He's my friend. You're my boyfriend. I might hug him, but that's it. He doesn't get the rest of me. You do, okay?"

"Do I?"

"You know you do." Josh's eyes started to drop, but I gripped the collar of his polo shirt, forcing him to look at me. "Hey, okay?"

"Maybe you should show me." He grinned, and his tone was light, but his words did something funny to my insides. Not in the way they were supposed to though.

He must have noticed my smile slip because he quickly added, "Shit, that came out all wrong. I didn't mean it. Crap, Dayna, you know I'll wait until you're ready."

"I know." I pecked him again, brushing it off. "I should go up to my room before Dad comes and checks on us. I'll see you tomorrow, okay?"

Josh pouted, his cute puppy dog eyes making me feel a tad guilty for leaving. "I love you, Dayna; you know that, right?"

"I know. I love you too. Sleep tight." I blew him a kiss and walked to the door, closing it behind me. It clicked shut, but I didn't move. I needed a second to catch my breath. I knew Josh didn't mean anything by his flippant remark, but it didn't change the fact we still hadn't had sex.

At first, it was because I was nervous, inexperienced. Now, eight months later, I was just stalling. He knew it. I knew it. And I was pretty sure our small group of college friends knew it. But it was a big step for me, and I wanted to be one hundred and ten percent sure before we did it.

Because ninety-nine percent just didn't seem good enough.

CHAPTER 3

DAYNA

"DID YOU TWO HAVE FUN TODAY?" Mom asked, ushering us up to the breakfast counter.

"We did," I said, helping myself to one of her special recipe chili-cheese coneys. "We visited the beach and checked out the Marblehead Lighthouse; then we got lunch at Clams."

"Sounds very romantic," she beamed.

"It was nice."

"Good to be back, I bet."

"So good. I love the city, but there's something comforting about being back in Dupont Beach."

"And what do you think of our little slice of heaven, Josh?"

"It's nice," he said, "but it's not somewhere I can ever see myself settling down."

Mom's brows furrowed as she cast me a questioning glance, and my spine went rigid. "Not a fan of small-town life?" she asked with a tightness in her voice that hadn't been there before.

"It's okay for vacations and fly-by visits, sure. But I can't see us putting down roots somewhere like Dupont Beach. Right, babe?" Josh patted my hand, and I forced a smile.

"I see. Well, it's always been enough for us."

"Oh, no, Mrs. Benson, I meant no offense." He dazzled her with a smile, but it did little to ease the knot in my stomach. "Dupont Beach is very charming. But I'm a city boy at heart."

"And how is that going to work—"

A knock at the back door drew Mom's attention, and Carson stuck his head inside. "Hey, hope I'm not interrupting anything?"

"Not at all, sweetie. Come on in. I made chili-cheese coneys."

"Mmm, my favorite."

"Take a seat, and I'll get one plated up for you."

"You're the best, Judy. So what have you two lovebirds been up to?"

"Dayna wanted to show me around," Josh said. "Dupont Beach is quite something."

Huh. Not what he said two minutes ago.

"Nowhere else like it on Earth. A place like Dupont Beach steals your heart and refuses to give it back. Why do you think Dayna is moving ho—"

"Here you go, sweetheart." Mom's impeccable timing saved us from moving the conversation into awkward territory.

Because Carson was right—I had moved back to Dupont Beach, and Josh didn't see himself ever settling down here. And I think some part of me knew that.

Maybe even banked on it.

God, what was wrong with me? Josh was perfect; he was. Smart and sexy and a real boy-next-door type. But something was missing. Or maybe, the parts of me that were meant to swoon and melt at a guy like Josh loving a girl like me were broken.

"This is really good, Judy," Carson tore into his chili-cheese coney, grinning at me like a fool.

"Pig," I said.

"Brat."

Josh cleared his throat. "I was thinking we could—"

The blare of Carson's cell phone cut through the

room. "Shit, sorry. It's Coach. He tried to call me earlier. I'll just take this outside." He got up and answered. "Coach Tucker, yeah, what do you need..."

The door closed behind him, drowning out his voice, and silence rippled through the kitchen.

"So he's like some hockey guru or something?"

"He's an assistant coach at Lakeshore U, the college a couple of towns over," I said.

"I've heard of it."

"It was always Dalton and Carson's dream to play for the Lakers and go pro. But then Carson got injured in his senior year, and it was enough to take him out of the draft. Coach Tucker didn't want to lose him, so he offered him a job."

"I've never really understood hockey."

"Oh, my goodness, how'd that work out for you during hockey season?" Mom asked, and he frowned.

"What do you mean?"

"Well, this one is a huge Blue Jacket fan."

"Mom," I hissed, giving my head a little shake.

"Dayna, what are you—"

"There wasn't a lot of time for all of that in Boston," I said, hoping she would drop it.

Hockey had been my life here; after Dalton died, that light inside me had blinked out. I'd thrown myself into other things at college—less painful things.

Of course, whenever I came home—and it hadn't been all that much in the last four years—I was thrust right back into the heart of it. But in Boston, it was different.

I was different there.

Maybe a little too much.

"I'm more of a baseball guy." Josh smiled, but it didn't reach his eyes.

Back in Boston, it had been easy to get lost in him, in his plans for the future. But from the second we got in the car, our differences only grew more and more apparent with every passing mile.

Now it felt like there was an ocean between us, and I wasn't sure what to do.

Carson came back inside, and I immediately asked, "What's wrong?"

He blew out a strained breath and ran his hand down his face. "Coach needs a favor."

"That doesn't sound so bad."

His expression tightened as he said, "He wants Aiden Dumfries to stay with me for the summer."

"Aiden Dumfries?" I blanched. "The Lakers hotheaded center? But isn't he from Detroit?"

"He ran into some trouble and needs to lie low for a few weeks."

"Surely that's not your responsibility, Cars."

"It's not. But Coach knows I have plenty of room at the house, and I'm someone Aiden knows and trusts."

"Aiden Dumfries... why does that name sound familiar?" Josh asked, glancing between the two of us.

"He was in the news," I said, my stomach sinking. "His father is Dawson Dumfries."

"Dawson Dumfries." He blanched. "The con artist from Detroit?"

"One and the same," Carson said tightly.

"Well, you know what I always say," Mom interjected. "You can't judge a son by the sins of his father."

"Pretty sure the Bible said that and not you, Mom." I smiled despite the uneasiness I felt.

"I put my own spin on it." She smiled back. "It sounds like Aiden needs somebody to guide him right, and I couldn't think of a better person." Squeezing Carson's arm, she went back to the dirty dishes.

"I don't like it, Dayna," Josh whispered. "Everyone knows Dawson Dumfries is bad news, and it sounds like Aiden is a chip off the old block. Maybe you should come with me to Toledo."

"I'll be fine. Aiden isn't coming to stay with me. Besides, my mom is right," I said. "We don't know anything about him."

Except, I'd heard the stories. Seen the headlines. He was the bad boy of Division I hockey.

And he was coming to stay with Carson for the whole summer.

I understood Josh's hesitation, but it wasn't like me and Carson would be spending that much time together. I started my internship in a couple of weeks, and Carson was helping his dad out with their family fishing charter business.

Josh gave me a tight-lipped smile.

"Don't worry, man," Carson said, obviously catching the end of our conversation. "I'll look out for her."

"I'm sure you will." Josh stiffened. "Excuse me; I'm going to check in with my folks." He walked out of the kitchen, taking the air with him.

I glared at Carson, and he recoiled, "What?"

"Really, you had to throw fuel on the fire?"

"It's not my fault if Josh is feeling a tad insecure."

"Carson Walsh," Mom chided with a knowing smile.

"I'd better go talk to him," I said.

"Oh, come on, Bug, I was joking," he called after me.

But I kept going.

Not sparing him a second glance.

"Hey." I slipped into the guest room and closed the door behind me.

"Hey." Josh was perched on the edge of the bed; his head hung low.

"You know you don't have to worry about me, right? This is my home, Josh."

"I know. But I can't help but think I'm going to lose you. You have this life here... this life that I know nothing about. Doesn't that strike you as odd?"

I went and sat down beside him. "You knew I planned on coming home after graduation." It was time. I'd spent far too long hiding in Boston. "You said you were okay with it."

"I know, and I get it. I do. You have a great opportunity here, and it's your home. But I guess I need to know that you'll choose me once you've gotten it out of your system."

"Excuse me?" The room contracted around me.

"Shit, that's not..." He released a long breath. "That came out wrong. I just want to know this isn't permanent. That you see a life beyond this place. With me."

"Josh, we've been together for eight months."

"And I love you, Dayna." He ran his hand along the side of my neck. "I love you, and I see a life with you. But not here, not in a place like this. I'm not cut out for small-town living."

"What are you saying?" I pulled back, blinking at him.

"Look, maybe some space will be a good thing. We can both take some time to figure out what we want and whether our paths are on the same trajectory."

"The same trajectory... And if they're not? If I don't fit into your plans, you want to break up?" Disbelief coated my words, a strange sinking feeling going through me.

"No, no, Dayna. I love you, babe." He kissed me. "But maybe we want different things, after all."

"And you've decided that after being here for what, a couple of days?" Tears pricked the corners of my eyes. "That isn't fair, and you know it. My life here is... complicated."

"Which is why I think some time apart will be good."

"This is really how you want to leave things? You head to Toledo tomorrow."

He kissed my forehead. "College is over, babe. It's time to go out into the real world and live."

His words felt like another dig. Did he think that by coming back home, I was still hiding?

I wasn't.

Coming back here wasn't easy. Not when everywhere I looked, I was reminded of Dalton. But I had ghosts here. Ghosts I needed to lay to rest. I thought Josh understood that.

I thought he got it.

"Fine, if that's what you want," I said, confused at how we'd gone from spending an amazing day exploring together to... to *this*.

"It'll be a good thing, you'll see."

I wasn't so sure about that, but I wasn't about to beg either.

"Do you still want to go to dinner?" I asked flatly. "We have a reservation with my parents."

At my favorite seafood restaurant overlooking the lake.

"Of course, I do. It's our last night together for a while. I want it to be special."

I stared at him, confusion trickling through me.

Special.

He sure could have fooled me.

"Thank you for a lovely evening, Mr. and Mrs. Benson," Josh said as we made our way into the house.

It was strange how genuine his words seemed after our conversation earlier. Tonight, he'd sat with my parents, listening to their stories of small-town living, and smiled and nodded in all the right places. But I couldn't unhear his words. *Maybe some space will be a good thing.* Because his actions tonight—his hand clasped around mine, toying with the ends of my hair—hadn't suggested space. Far from it.

"You won't get a better shrimp than Pearls," Dad said, pulling me back into the moment.

"Oh, I don't know about that. My mom makes a mean shrimp scampi."

"She does? A woman after my own heart."

"Hey, mister." Mom slapped Dad's chest.

"Your scampi is good too, Judy." Their laughter filled the hall. "Well, it's late. So we'll say good night. Sorry we won't be around to see you off in the morning, Josh." Dad held out his hand. "But it's been really nice meeting you, son."

"You too, sir—"

"Derek, call me Derek. Hopefully, we'll be seeing you again soon." Dad glanced between the two of us, and my stomach dipped.

"I sure hope so."

"Josh." Mom pulled him in for a hug. "It's been so good to finally meet you."

"You too, Judy."

"Don't be a stranger, okay? You might be a city boy at heart, but you'll always be welcome here. Night, sweetheart."

"Night, Mom," I said, "Dad."

They headed upstairs, leaving Josh and me alone.

"Come on," I said, taking his hand and leading him down the hall to his room. We slipped inside, and I turned to face him, trailing a shaky finger up his chest. "So I was thinking," my voice trembled, "we could—"

"Dayna," he sighed, gently removing my hand. "Your parents." His gaze went to the door.

"They'll be out for the count in like ten minutes. And besides, this room is at the back of the house. I thought it might be nice if we... spend the night together before you leave."

I leaned in, kissing the corner of his mouth, nervous energy zipping through me.

All night I'd gone back and forth over our conver-

sation and come to the conclusion that Josh was right
—I couldn't keep stalling. He loved me, and I cared a
lot about him. It was just sex. Everyone did it eventually. And doing it the night before he left seemed
romantic.

Special.

It felt like it would bring us closer together and
erase all the doubts and worries we both had.

"Josh," I murmured against his lips. "I want this. I
want you." I went to wrap my arms around him, but he
gently gripped my wrists, holding me at bay.

"Not tonight, babe. It's late, I'm tired, and I have a
busy day tomorrow." He gave me an apologetic smile.

"Oh, okay." My stomach dropped, dejection
curdling inside me.

Had I really just offered to sleep with my boyfriend
for the first time, and he turned me down?

I stepped back, not knowing where to look. "Well,
this is awkward." Strained laughter bubbled out of me
as I stared at the floor, wanting to disappear
through it.

"Hey." Josh pulled me into his arms and slid his
fingers under my jaw, coaxing my face up to his. "I love
you, Dayna. And I can wait for you, okay?"

"Okay."

But his words didn't soothe the knot in my stomach. Because he'd been waiting for months now, and more than once, he'd made his impatience known.

It didn't make any sense.

An awkward silence lingered between us, but he made no effort to reassure me any further, so I said, "I guess I'll see you in the morning."

"Okay, babe." He kissed me on the cheek. "Maybe we can get breakfast before I leave."

"Sure."

Josh gave me a crooked grin before ushering me to the door. He held it open, a clear sign he wanted me to leave.

So I walked out of there alone.

Wondering what the hell had just happened.

CHAPTER 4

DAYNA

> Josh: Made it here in one piece.
> Things are kind of crazy, so I'll call
> you later. Love you. xo

I reread the text message again, trying to dissect every word. Josh had left this morning, and to say things had been awkward, was an understatement.

On the one hand, he'd hugged me tight, his hand buried in my hair as he whispered how much he loved me, how he was already counting the days until he saw me again. But on the other, he'd planted this giant seed of doubt between us.

He wanted us to have some space—what did that even mean?

We were in a long-distance relationship, for Pete's sake. You didn't get much more space than that. But I'd been too confused—too dejected—to push for an answer over breakfast this morning. So, I'd watched him climb into his car and disappear down the road, leaving an empty, hollow feeling spreading through me.

"Bug?" Carson's voice filled the house, and I let out a heavy sigh, dropping my cell on the coffee table.

"In here," I called.

He appeared a second later. But he wasn't alone.

My gaze landed on his friend, and he cut me with an icy glare. I quickly averted my eyes, surprised by the animosity in his dark gaze.

"Hey, I just wanted to drop by and introduce you to Aiden. He arrived this morning."

Tension rippled between the two of them. I'd caught the odd photo of Aiden Dumfries in the Daily Puck, my favorite hockey blog, but none of them did justice to his cold demeanor.

He was tall, taller than I imagined, at least six foot two, and his biceps were huge, corded with muscle, and covered in ink.

"Hi," I said, dragging my gaze away from him. "Welcome to Dupont Beach."

"Hey," he replied flatly.

No hint of a smile, fake or otherwise.

Well, okay then.

My eyes flashed to Carson, and he rubbed his jaw, hiding a grimace. "Aiden here wasn't too happy about being shipped off to stay with me. But I told him Dupont Beach isn't so bad. Dayna actually just moved home from Boston too. So you two have that in common."

Aiden barely reacted, a wall of hostility radiating around him. He was as cold as ice, nothing like Carson or Josh. But there was something about the way he watched me—that cold, unforgiving stare biting into my skin.

Burning.

"Anyway," Carson's voice jolted me from the strange pull I felt toward Aiden. "We're on our way to The Spot for some lunch before I give him the grand tour."

I wanted to say, 'good luck with that.' Instead, I smiled and said, "Have fun."

Aiden made a small derisive noise in the back of his throat. He was gorgeous, no denying that. But he was clearly an ass.

"Here," Carson threw his keys at his new house-mate. "Go wait in the truck. I'll be right there."

Relief etched into Aiden's expression, and he walked out of the room without so much as a goodbye.

The back door slammed shut, and I flinched. "He seems... friendly."

Carson let out a heavy sigh, his gaze on the door. "Coach Tucker must really fucking hate me to send him here for the summer."

"Or he knows you can handle it," I shot back.

"Yeah, maybe." His eyes flicked to the door and back to me. "Josh get off okay?"

"Yeah, fine," I said, a little too hastily.

Carson noticed, frowning. "What's wrong?"

"Nothing."

"Bug..."

"Don't you need to get back to your babysitting duties?"

"Nah, he can wait a minute. Besides, I'll always have time for you. Trouble in Josh paradise?"

"Cars." I rolled my eyes.

"What?"

"You know what. He's a good guy."

"I'm sure he is... he's just not the kind of guy I ever imagined you with."

"What's that supposed to mean?" I recoiled.

"He doesn't even like hockey, Bug."

"That doesn't mean we're not compatible."

"True. But call it a gut feeling."

"A gut feeling." I stood, needing to do something. "How very intuitive of you."

"Come on, don't be like that. I guess I just always pictured you with someone with the same interests and values."

"You don't know anything about him, so I don't think you really get to have an opinion."

Carson stood too, running a hand down his face. "And why is that?" His brow arched, his expression full of accusation and disappointment.

"That's not fair, and you know it." Anger trickled down my spine.

So maybe I hadn't been upfront about Josh. Maybe I'd hidden behind my parents, letting them break the news to him, but it was only because I was trying to live my life for myself. To find me again after losing Dalton. My relationship with Carson was so deeply entwined with my grief that I'd pulled away because I needed to stand on my own two feet again.

I had to prove to myself I could function without him.

He exhaled a thin breath. "I need to go. But we'll talk about this later."

"Whatever," I said.

It wasn't the most mature comeback, but he'd

caught me off guard. And if I was being honest with myself, his words rang too true. Josh and I weren't well-suited. But weren't opposites supposed to attract? Just because he was a city boy at heart and a part of me would always belong in Dupont Beach didn't mean we couldn't make it work.

Except he wants space and didn't want you last night.

A sticky trail of dejection snaked through me.

"Bug?"

"Just go, Carson. I'll talk to you later."

His expression softened, guilt shining in his eyes. But he started backing away. "I'll call you later."

I won't answer.

I needed some time to figure things out. Being home was turning out to be more difficult than I thought. But not for the reasons I expected.

I thought I'd be sad, too crippled with grief to come back here. But it wasn't that at all. My past and present had intersected by bringing Josh home with me.

And maybe they weren't compatible after all.

"Hey, it's me," I said. "I tried calling you earlier, but there was no answer. I hope you're settling in. Maybe you're out, or something, or maybe your reception is bad. Just... call me when you get this."

Hanging up, I shoved my cell phone into my pocket and stared out at the lake. The dusky pink sunset reflecting off the water was beautiful this time of year.

It was one of the things I'd missed most while living in Boston.

My heart squeezed.

"God, I miss you," I murmured to the breeze.

"Miss who?"

A deep voice startled me, and I glanced up to find Aiden Dumfries staring down at me.

"Uh, no one."

"Your brother, right? Dalton Benson? One of the best right-wingers the NCAA had ever seen. Can I?" He motioned to the sand beside me, and before I could answer, he dropped down.

"Sure, make yourself comfortable," I murmured.

"Don't mind if I do." He smirked.

Aiden Dumfries smirked at me, and I sat there gawking at him. Because he was so at odds with the guy I'd met earlier, I felt like I'd landed in the middle of the *Twilight Zone*.

"Where's Carson?"

He lifted a shoulder in a small shrug as he stared out at the lake. "His old man called and needed a hand with something. Left me at the house, so I wandered down here."

"Carson talked to you... about Dalton?"

"Hell no. Carson barely talks to any of us about Dalton. But we all know the story. We all know it's why he didn't go pro."

"Oh." My chest constricted.

At the time, Carson had said he didn't go into the draft because of an injury, but I'd always known it was because Dalton was gone.

"So, are the two of you like... a thing?"

"What?" My eyes almost bugged out. "God no, Carson is like a brother to me. Why would you say that?"

"Picked up on some vibes earlier between the two of you."

"We're close." At least we used to be. "But it isn't like that."

"Cool," he said, sliding his cool gaze to mine. The air crackled around us, a strange sensation curling in my stomach. His hand reached for me, toying with the ends of my hair.

"What are—"

Aiden leaned in and kissed me, his body coming down on mine, forcing my back into the sand. I was so shocked, so freaking confused, that I lost myself in the kiss for a second. In how his mouth felt, how his hot breath mingled with mine as he flicked his tongue along the seam of my lips. A small gasp left me, and he took that as permission to plunge his tongue into my mouth.

Reality crashed over me, and I slammed my palms into his chest, shoving with all of my might. "What the hell are you doing?" I cried.

"The fuck?" His eyes narrowed, a wall slamming between us.

"You kissed me."

"And you pushed me away."

"I didn't say you could kiss me."

"You said you and Carson weren't—"

"We're not. But I have a boyfriend."

He rolled off me and flopped onto the sand, running a hand down his face.

Touching a finger to my lips, I inhaled a shaky breath. "Do you always kiss random girls?"

"I'm not sure you want to know the answer to that."

"Oh."

A sinking feeling went through me, which was really freaking weird. Aiden had just kissed me—

without permission. Anger was a more appropriate response, and maybe a little part of me was angry. But there was something else, something I didn't want to acknowledge because I had a boyfriend.

Josh.

Oh God, Josh.

Guilt rose up inside me like a tidal wave. "You kissed me," I blurted again.

"Are you going to keep saying that? Because it's kind of annoying."

"You're annoying."

"You're freaking out." He peeked up at me.

"You kissed me, and I have a boyfriend."

"It was just a little kiss, freckles. Don't get your panties in a twist."

"Don't talk about my panties, and don't call me freckles." I flushed with irritation. *Freckles.* Pfft. It made me sound like a child. "You can't just go around kissing people without their permission."

"Usually, they don't mind."

"Oh my God," I breathed. "You need to go."

"Go? But I just got here."

"And now you need to leave."

"Carson didn't say you were this weird."

"Me?" I shrieked. "I'm not the one who goes around kissing people without their permission."

He groaned, covering his face with his arm.

"Aiden, I'm serious. You need to leave."

"Sorry, I can't hear you."

Tears of frustration pricked the corner of my eyes. What the hell was happening? I'd gone from wallowing on the beach to kissing Aiden Dumfries, the Lakeshore U Lakers bad boy of hockey.

"Fine. If you don't leave, I will."

"Over dramatic, much. It was just one little kiss. Relax, freckles, I've already forgotten about it."

His words socked me in the stomach—first Josh's rejection and now Aiden's dismissal. Coming back to Dupont Beach had so far done a real number on my self-esteem.

"Wow," I spat, clambering to my feet. "You know I'm a firm believer in not believing everything you read about somebody in the press. About giving someone the benefit of the doubt. But I guess this time, they were pretty damn accurate."

He pulled his arm away and glared up at me. "You don't know the first fucking thing about me."

"Good, something tells me I don't want to." I spun on my heel and stormed off up the beach.

How dare he.

How dare he come down here and insert himself

into my sanctuary and then kiss me and act like it was nothing.

Before I could stop myself, I glanced back only to find he hadn't moved. He was still lying there, staring up at the sky. I needed to tell Josh and Carson. It wasn't right. He couldn't just go around kissing people like that.

A shiver ran through me. I wanted to believe it was disgust that I was so outraged by what had happened that my body was having a physical reaction.

But that was a lie.

Because it wasn't only outrage. It was something else.

Ugh.

As I headed back toward the house, I played over in my head how I would tell Josh. I'd done nothing wrong; I'd pushed Aiden away. I would just come clean and tell him.

But as the house appeared up ahead, my cell phone vibrated. I pulled it out.

Josh.

Dread snaked through me.

But it quickly turned to something pricklier when I opened the message.

Josh: Sorry I missed your call. Going out with my roommate so I'll call you tomorrow. Love you. xo

Tomorrow?

As I clutched my phone, I tried to tell myself it didn't mean anything, that he was just busy getting settled and finding his feet.

But as I let myself into the house, unshed tears burned my eyes.

He wanted space.

And he seemed determined to get it.

CHAPTER 5

AIDEN

"Where have you been?" Carson asked the second I stepped into his kitchen.

His house was a big, sprawling place overlooking Lake Erie. No wonder Coach Tucker had sent me out here. It was the perfect place to exile me.

"For a walk." His brow lifted at that, and I added, "Don't worry, I didn't get into any trouble."

Much anyway.

My mind instantly went to his friend, Dayna Benson.

Shit, I shouldn't have kissed her, but she was looking at me all doe-eyed and cute, and before I knew it, I'd pressed my mouth to hers.

Girls at Lakeshore U didn't usually care. I was Aiden fucking Dumfries. The guy everyone wanted to know. The guy that girls tripped over themselves to get a piece of.

It was just one little kiss, and she'd acted like I'd tried to fuck her.

Little Miss Prude.

Carson narrowed his eyes. "What's up with you?"

"What? Nothing." I barged past him, heading for the kitchen.

"You know, it's going to be a long summer if you don't talk to me about it."

"Nothing to say."

"Aiden, man, come on."

Fuck. The guy was like a dog with a bone. All day, he'd been trying to get me to talk. I didn't want to fucking talk. I wanted to do my time out here, go back to college for my final year with the Lakers, and forget all about my piece of a shit sperm donor.

It wasn't my fault I drew the short straw in the father lottery.

Dawson Dumfries was nobody to me.

Nothing.

Yet, his reputation haunted me like a spirit that refused to move on to the afterlife.

"You are not your father," he said.

"Yeah, well, try telling that to the residents of Monroe."

"Talk to me. What happened?" He leaned against the counter, arms folded over his chest.

"Some asshole was running his mouth in the diner where my mom works. I asked him to stop. Twice. The third time, I lost it."

"You broke his nose."

"Yeah, well," I clenched a fist, wincing at the bite of pain across my tender knuckles. "I should have done a whole lot worse than that."

"Coach barely kept your ass out of jail."

"What do you want me to say?" I shrugged. "He was disrespecting my mom. I'm not just going to standby and take that shit."

She'd been through enough.

"There are other ways…"

"Yeah, okay. So you're telling me you wouldn't break some fuckers nose if he were talking shit about your mom or Dayna."

"Dayna?" His brows crinkled. "What's she got to do with anything?"

"I just figured you two are close?"

What the fuck? I didn't care about his relationship with Dayna. Didn't care that she'd shoved me away like I was some creeper. Which I guess, when you thought about it, I was.

I hadn't meant to kiss her. But she was pretty, all those sun-kissed freckles taunting me every time she smiled, and aside from being on the ice, getting down and dirty with a girl was the best fucking distraction there was.

But she was important to Carson, and he was important to the team—the team I needed if I was going to turn pro.

For fuck's sake.

I'd come close to screwing up today. But that was my middle name.

Aiden 'the screwup' Dumfries.

Nobody actually called me that, but it sure felt like they did. Partly because I was Dawson Dumfries' kid, partly because I was a hotheaded cocky fucker that had a ton of trust issues and struggled with authority.

"Dayna is family. And too fucking good for the likes of you, Dumfries, so don't go getting any ideas."

Anger rolled up my spine. But he was right. Of course, she was too good for a guy like me.

"Dalton's sister," I said. "That's got to be rough."

Jesus, I had no filter today.

"We're not talking about Dalton or Dayna. Mom sent some leftovers if you're hungry. Tomorrow we've been invited over to the Bensons' for a cookout."

"I'll pass."

"Like hell, you will." He scowled. "The Bensons are good people."

Not sure Dayna would want me coming around after earlier, but it wasn't like I could tell Carson that.

"I'm not looking to make friends, Coach."

"And maybe that's your damn problem. You think I haven't noticed how you keep people at arm's length? Your teammates, the coaching staff at LU."

"I'm a team player," I said defensively.

"Yeah, and a good one. But you don't let people get close."

Too right, I didn't. If people got close, if you let them in, they tended to hurt you. And I was done being taken for a fool by people.

"Thanks for the pep talk, Coach," I spat the words, heading for the door.

"Tomorrow Aiden," he called after me. "I expect you to be there."

The Benson yard was the last place I wanted to be. But Carson Walsh wouldn't let it drop. He'd let me sleep in. The note he'd left on the refrigerator informed me he was helping his mom and dad again for a few hours. So I'd spent the day on his couch in my shorts, eating crackers out of the box and drinking the three beers he had stashed in his refrigerator. He'd taken one look at me when he got home, told me to get a shower and into some clean clothes, or he would call up Coach Tucker and make sure he knew just how productive his star player was spending his summer break.

Asshole.

"You can come and join us, you know, Aiden, sweetie," Mrs. Benson crooned as she wandered over to me and offered me a fresh drink.

"Thanks, Mrs. Benson," I said. "I'm just enjoying the scenery." My eyes flicked to the beach in the near distance, the vast sparkling body of Lake Erie.

It really was something, especially as the sun shone down over it. A strange sense of peace I rarely felt went through me as I stood there, taking it all in. Monroe was a coastal town, but we didn't have a view of the lake from our small house.

"I'll never tire of that," she said with a soft, contented sigh. "But come and join us. This is supposed to be a family meal, and we've already lost Dayna to her phone."

I scanned their yard, and sure enough, Little Miss Prude was missing.

"I think it's Josh," Mrs. Benson went on, talking as if we were old friends. "It sounded strained."

"Josh, the boyfriend?"

She nodded. "Nice young man but not cut out for small-town life apparently."

"He doesn't know what he's missing."

I don't know why I said it, but the words were out now, and Mrs. Benson was beaming at me.

"I'm quite inclined to agree. Oh well, his loss. Now come on, the steak is almost cooked."

"Sure, why not." The food did smell good, and my diet of crackers and beer hadn't exactly filled me up. I would need to increase my workout tomorrow to burn the extra calories.

"Carson tells me you got yourself into a spot of trouble back home," Mr. Benson said, flipping the steaks onto a huge plate.

"Something like that." I shot Carson a hard look, and he smirked.

"Derek is as good as family and a huge hockey fan."

"Damn right, I am. Rumor has it, you've got a shot at going all the way."

"That's the plan, sir," I said, taking a pull on my

beer. Carson had tried to give me a soda when we first arrived, but Mrs. Benson had shooed him away and gotten me a real drink.

Thank fuck.

"You got a team in sight, son?"

"The dream would be the Red Wings."

"Spoken like any true Detroiter." He smiled. "Better knuckle down next season and show the scouts what you've got."

"Been telling him that for the past year," Carson said. "But hey, what do I know?"

I rolled my eyes, waiting for the full speech.

"He should have been captain last season, but we all know how that turned out."

I bristled. I'd known I was their first choice, but I'd screwed up the season before, getting into a fight after the final whistle blew that earned me a two-game suspension. There was no way Coach Tucker could name me captain after that, so I'd spent the season licking my wounds and working on my temper.

"Cut the kid some slack, Carson. College is a lot of pressure. Throw in hopes of going pro one day, and it's enough to make any guy falter a little now and again. What's important is stepping up when it counts." Mr. Benson pinned me with a knowing look. "Something tells me this is your year, son."

"Sure, do hope so, sir."

I wanted it. Had fucking dreamed of it since I was a kid, skating out on Lake Monroe in my hand-me-down skates and pads.

Hockey was my life, my shot at proving myself. But Mr. Benson was right; the pressure was, at times, unbearable. And I did crumble under the weight of it.

I drained my beer and wiped my mouth with the back of my hand. Carson's gaze narrowed at me as if he knew all the doubts and dark thoughts running through my head.

"Derek is right, you know. Next season is yours. You just have to reach out and take it. I'm talking a one-way ticket into the Frozen Four and getting the call-up from the pros.

"No distractions. No screw ups. Just one hundred and ten percent focus."

"Yeah, yeah, Coach. I know the drill."

And come the new semester, I fully intended to stick to the plan.

Although if the night carried on like this, I was going to need something a little stronger than beer.

"Oh, Dayna sweetheart, there you— What's wrong?" Mrs. Benson rushed over to her daughter as she approached.

"Nothing, Mom, I'm fine." Dayna smiled, but it didn't reach her eyes.

"Is it Josh—"

"I said I'm fine." She glanced over at us, and Carson cleared his throat.

"Smells good, Derek."

"It's all in the marinade," he said, giving the women some privacy. But I kept glancing over at them, drawn to Dayna, her closed-off posture, and the way she pressed the tip of her thumb against her lips.

"Dumfries," Carson growled, and my eyes snapped to his. "It's rude to stare."

"Fuck you," I mouthed, and he snorted.

"Come on. Let's dig in." Mr. Benson placed the plate down in the middle of the table, which was already full of food. Salad and potatoes and freshly baked bread. It was a real feast, and it felt weird as fuck to sit down with them.

They were clearly close. Had obviously done this a lot over the years. Carson helped Mrs. Benson hand out mismatched plates and silverware with easy familiarity while Dayna filled everyone's glasses with freshly made lemonade.

I'd never had this. Family—blood or made— laughing and talking over a meal. My childhood was filled with disappointment and heartache, the kind that hardened your heart and blackened your soul.

"Everything okay, sweetheart?" Mr. Benson asked Dayna, and she nodded.

"Everything's fine, Dad."

Another tight-lipped smile that didn't reach her eyes.

Clearly, she was lying, but it wasn't my place to push her, and she didn't owe me anything.

Shit. I shouldn't have come here, trying to fit into their happy little family and play nice. Carson knew me well enough that he knew I didn't know how to do this—to be the kind of guy who charmed people with stories from my past.

"This steak sure smells good." Carson helped himself to one and loaded his plate with salad and potatoes.

"Best damn steak in the whole town of Dupont Beach." Mr. Benson turned his attention to his daughter again. "Are you looking forward to starting your internship, Dayna Bug?"

"I am."

"When do you start?" Carson asked.

"Not until the week after next."

"We'll have to take the boat out for old time's sake. Give Aiden a lesson on the water."

"I'm good staying on dry land," I said, digging into my food.

"Nonsense," Mrs. Benson scoffed. "You won't find a better teacher than Carson. He and Dalton taught Dayna everything she knows."

A heavy silence fell over the table.

"Dalton sure did love to go out on the lake," Carson's voice cracked.

I was an intruder here in their moment of shared grief, and I didn't know what the fuck to do.

"Excuse me," Dayna shot up out of her seat. "I... I need to use the bathroom." She took off without another word, and Mr. Benson let out a heavy sigh.

"I'll go after her."

"No," he said to his wife. "Leave her be. It will always be tough on her, coming back here."

Carson stared up at the house, pain shining in his eyes, but he didn't move to go after her either.

"I'm sorry about that, Aiden."

"You don't need to apologize, Mr. Benson. I'm the one who feels like they're intruding."

"Nonsense, any friend of Carson's, is welcome at our table. Besides, it isn't every day you get to meet a future NHL star." He winked.

"Oh, I don't know about that, sir." I dropped my eyes, pushing the salad around my plate.

"If Carson here says you can go all the way, then I believe him."

I glanced over at Carson, and he smirked. "Don't look so surprised, Dumfries. You know you're good. The Lakers haven't seen a center with your skill and playmaking on the ice since... well, my era." His smirk turned smug.

"You were okay, I guess."

Mr. Benson whistled through his teeth. "You were good, Carson, son; I'll give you that. Would have shined in the pros too, but I think Aiden has something extra."

"Something extra, huh?"

The two of them stared at me like I didn't want the ground to open up and swallow me whole. I knew I was good, but there was still one season ahead of me —the most important season of my life.

"Yeah, but..."

"But nothing," Carson said. "You just need to keep your nose out of trouble and keep your eye on the prize."

"The Stanley Cup," Mr. Benson added.

"He's right, you know. The world is your oyster, Dumfries." Carson pinned me with a hard look. One that said he wouldn't go easy on me this season. "You just have to want it enough."

"Yeah, yeah, save me the speech, old man."

Mr. and Mrs. Benson laughed, but I saw the shadows in their eyes.

They matched the ones in their daughter's.

CHAPTER 6

AIDEN

DAYNA DIDN'T RETURN. Mrs. Benson went to check on her and came back five minutes later with a grim expression and a whispered word for her husband.

Carson didn't ask, and neither did I.

"So, how are you enjoying Dupont Beach so far, Aiden?" Mr. Benson asked as we sat around the fire pit. It was summer, but the air turned cooler as soon as the sun sank beneath the horizon.

"I haven't really had time to explore yet."

"Well, if you need a tour guide. I'm sure Dayna would be willing to show you all the local hotspots."

"I'm sure she's got better things to do than—"

"Nonsense." He waved me off. "I'll ask her tomorrow."

I murmured a non-committal response. Dayna wouldn't want to show me around any more than I wanted her to.

"Who wants some homemade fudge?" Mrs. Benson and Carson appeared with more drinks and food. I was going to roll back to Carson's at this rate, and I wasn't here to relax and enjoy the summer break. I was here to lay low and work on my fitness, getting ready for the new season.

"Actually, I'm good, thanks," I said, standing. "Can I use your bathroom before we leave?"

"Leave, but it's still early." Mrs. Benson protested.

"Aiden's right, Judy. I have an early start again, and the last thing Aiden needs is to become a couch potato over the summer."

"I suppose you're right. Sure, you go on in, sweetheart. It's the last door down the hall."

"Thanks."

I made my way up to the house, my eyes flicking to the first-floor windows. Dayna was in one of those rooms, and I couldn't help but wonder if she was hiding.

Moving through the kitchen into the hall, I noted

the photos. The Bensons and their perfect family. Except, it wasn't perfect, was it?

They'd lost a son. Dayna had lost her brother.

These people knew loss. They knew grief and pain and heartache.

I knew loss too, but it wasn't the same. My sperm donor hadn't died. He'd chosen a life of easy money and screwing people over instead of his family. Me. Some days, I wished he was dead. It would be a damn sight easier than living in his shadow.

I found the bathroom and quickly took care of business. I needed to get out of here. The Bensons were good people, too good for the likes of me. I didn't belong here. And I was going to have to tell Carson I wasn't looking to be adopted by them for the summer, no matter how welcomed they had made me feel.

After washing my hands, I slipped out of the bathroom and headed back down the hall. But Dayna's raised voice snagged my attention.

Before I could stop myself, I'd followed the sound to the foot of the stairs.

"What the hell, Josh? You didn't text me all day, and now you're calling me overemotional. Sorry if I wanted to talk to my boyfriend... What, no, I haven't been drinking. What kind of question is that?" Her voice grew louder, and I ducked around the corner as she came downstairs. "I know you said we should have some space. I didn't think— fine. Fine, whatever." She headed for the kitchen, and I rubbed my jaw. I also needed to go back through the kitchen.

Fuck.

The back door slammed, reverberating through me, and I breathed a sigh of relief. She'd gone straight out back, so I figured the coast was clear. I swiped a bottle of water off the counter and stepped outside, almost walking straight into her.

"Crap, sorry. I didn't know—"

"Dayna?" I steadied her shoulders, a zap of electricity going through me. Dropping my hands, I stepped back, putting some space between us. "Let me guess. The boyfriend?"

"That's... none of your busi— wait"—her eyes widened—"were you listening to my conversation?"

"You weren't exactly quiet."

"Oh my God, that's... I don't even know what to say to that." She wrapped her arms around herself, glancing down at the ground.

"It wasn't like I was eavesdropping. I came out of the bathroom, and you were coming downstairs." The lie rolled off my tongue, but something told me she wouldn't appreciate the truth. And I wasn't looking to get my balls handed to me by a hormonal female.

So why couldn't I walk the fuck away?

"Yeah, well, if you could just stay out of my business, that would be great." Her eyes flickered to mine, and I realized she was crying. She let out a weary sigh and went to move past me, but I grabbed her arm. "Aiden," she breathed, her eyes boring into mine.

"He doesn't deserve your tears."

What the fuck?

Where the hell had that come from?

Dayna stared at me—through me—and then snatched her arm away. "What are you doing?" she seethed.

"Excuse me?"

"Well, first you tried to kiss me, and now you're trying to give me relationship advice?"

"Relax, I'm not—"

"Dayna, sweetheart, are you coming to join us?" Mrs. Benson's voice cut through the air, and the tension swirling around us like a knife.

"Uh, sure, Mom. I'll be right there." Pain flickered across her expression.

"Look, Dayna, I wasn't—"

"Just... stay away from me, Aiden." She took off down the yard and left me standing there.

Wondering what the fuck had just happened.

The next day, I woke to someone hammering Carson's door down.

"Carson, man, get the door," I yelled, rolling over to grab my phone.

Shit.

It was past nine-thirty. Carson was already long gone.

I shoved back the sheet with a frustrated groan and padded downstairs to open the fucking door.

"What the hell— You," I said, lifting a brow at Dayna.

"Hey." She lifted her hand in a small wave. "I come bearing apology muffins."

"You made me apology muffins?"

"No, my mom made them, and I decided to dub them apology muffins. I was a bitch last night."

"You don't owe me anything." I shrugged, running a hand through my bed hair and down the back of my neck.

Dayna's gaze dropped to my bare chest, moving lower and lower until she was staring at my very noticeable morning wood.

"Uh, shit," I shoved my hand there, trying to disguise the impossible.

But I couldn't deny I liked the feel of her eyes on me or the slight flush to her cheeks as she brazenly checked me out.

Maybe freckles wasn't so innocent after all.

Interesting.

But she had a boyfriend, and one thing I didn't ever do, was get tangled up with a girl who had a boyfriend. It was too messy.

"You really like muffins, huh?" A shy smile traced her lips, but I saw the heat in her gaze.

"I literally just woke up. It's simple biology."

"Sure, keep telling yourself that." Her smile grew.

Yeah. I liked her like this. Flirting and playful and gazing at me with subtle interest in her eyes.

Stop, asshole. She isn't available.

"So can I come in, or do I have to stand out here all morning?"

"I... uh, you're coming in?"

That was fucking news to me.

"I am." She nodded. "If you move aside and let me in."

With little choice, I stepped back, and Dayna slipped past me, moving down Carson's hall. Something about the way she acted, as if she knew this house almost as well as her own, bothered me more than it should.

"Is there coffee?"

"You'll need to make a fresh pot," I replied, traipsing after her.

I wasn't awake enough for this. Her. The apology muffins.

"I can do that." She placed the container on the counter and turned on the coffee machine. "Creamer? Sugar?"

"Black, please."

"Why am I not surprised?" There was that smile again, but I didn't take the bait.

I cleared my throat, "Don't take this the wrong way, but what are you doing here?"

"You can blame my parents for that. They seem to think you need yourself a tour guide since Carson is busy."

"I don't."

"Which is exactly what I told them." She let out a little huff of irritation. "But in case you hadn't noticed, my parents can be very persuasive. Besides, I do feel bad about being rude to you."

"Yeah, well, like I said, you don't owe me anything."

"Are you always this hospitable?"

"Before ten in the morning and at least two strong coffees? You bet your ass I am."

"I thought all college athletes had to stick to a strict diet and off-season training regime."

"Do I look like I need a strict diet and training regime?" Unable to resist, I ran a hand down my six-pack, and Dayna blushed. But she was right—I did have to stick to my training schedule, or Coach would kick my ass.

"Can you... uh, go put on a shirt or something?"

"Why? Do my abs make you uncomfortable?" I tensed my pecs, and her eyes turned to saucers.

Dayna spun around and pretended to make the coffee, but I caught the way the tips of her ears turned pink too.

Interesting.

"I'll be right back." I slipped out of the kitchen, grabbed my hoodie off the coatrack, and pulled it over my head before heading back. "Better?"

She glanced over, her eyes twinkling with amusement. "Much. Here." Dayna slid a mug of coffee toward me. "Muffin?"

"Sure, why not." The corner of my mouth tipped.

"You're in an awfully good mood."

"I can go back to being a grumpy asshole if you'd prefer?"

"No, no. I think I prefer this Aiden."

We shared another smile.

What the fuck was happening?

This wasn't me. I didn't hang out with girls, drinking coffee, and eating apology muffins. But Dayna and her family had some weird ability to pull you into their orbit. Like magnets. And there was something about the way she looked at me. It wasn't like the puck bunnies at college who all wanted their five minutes of fame with a Laker. They didn't care about who I was beyond the number nineteen jersey I wore and how many goals I scored.

"So, the boyfriend—"

"We are not talking about Josh," Her tone cooled. "Or about the fact you tried to kiss me."

"Fine. But I don't want to talk about hockey or why I've been exiled to Dupont Beach."

"Fine." She gave a little shrug, but I didn't miss the way her lips twitched. "Now eat, and drink up. I've got a whole day of sightseeing planned. You're going to need your energy."

"So, what do you think?" Dayna asked as we sat on the jetty, eating our ice cream cones and watching the boats come and go from the small dock.

"It's... quaint."

"Quaint? I guess I can live with that." She licked her ice cream, and I found myself transfixed on her tongue. The way it curled around the frozen chocolate mint chip, savoring every moment.

"Crap. Do I have something on my face?" she asked, jolting me out of my reverie.

"No, you're fine. I just..." Shit. I had nothing.

A knowing smirk tugged at the corner of her mouth. "Now we're even."

"Even?"

She grinned wider, taking another enthusiastic swipe of her ice cream. But the moment was gone the second her phone vibrated. Dayna dug it out of her pocket and frowned.

"Let me guess, the boyfriend?" I mumbled.

Her eyes narrowed as she read the text message, the color draining from her cheeks.

"Everything okay?" I asked, not that I really wanted to know. But it seemed like the polite thing to do after she had been an entertaining tour guide.

Patient, funny, and knowledgeable without being

overbearing, Dayna hadn't pushed me for anything I hadn't been willing to tell her.

We'd spent the day wandering around Dupont Beach. From Main Street to the docks to the lighthouse at the end of the beach. It beat being holed up at Carson's all day, that was for sure.

"He's busy again."

"He's in Toledo for work, right?" She nodded, and I added, "He didn't want to stay in Dupont Beach and commute in?"

"He's always dreamed of living and working in the city."

"And you didn't want to go?"

"I needed to come home." She regarded me for a second and then said, "What?"

"Nothing."

"It's getting late." Dayna's gaze dropped, and I sensed I'd overstepped. "We should probably head back."

"Uh, yeah. Sure." I stood, wiping my hands on my shorts.

We walked back in thick silence. Dayna was lost in her thoughts, and I didn't know what to say. We weren't friends. We weren't enemies either, but I didn't know enough about her or her relationship with Josh to stick my nose in.

Not that I wanted to.

I didn't.

But I didn't like seeing her sad either. And I fucking hated the awkward silence.

"Are you looking forward to starting your internship? It's at the local newspaper, right?"

She let out a heavy sigh, "You know, you don't have to do that."

"Do what?"

"Pretend to be interested," she said with a dismissive shrug. "I know you didn't want to come out with me today."

"Dayna, that's not—"

"It's fine. I get it. But I needed the distraction and I knew it would make my parents happy."

"Do you always do things to please other people?"

Her eyes snapped to mine. "Do you always ask annoying questions?"

"Is that what you think I'm doing?"

"Whatever, Aiden." Her pace quickened as she took the grassy embankment leading away from the dock toward the beach that backed onto the Bensons' house.

"You can find your way home from here, right?" she asked.

"Come on, freckles, don't be like that." I reached for her, but she dodged my hand.

"My parents want you to come for lunch tomorrow, but I'll tell them you're busy." She took off in a hurry.

"I'm not," I called after her, pissed that she was acting so stupid over nothing.

But Dayna didn't reply, and I didn't go after her.

CHAPTER 7

DAYNA

"Dayna Bug, is that you?" Mom called when I slipped into the kitchen.

"Yeah, Mom."

"How was your day? Did you and Aiden have fun?" She appeared at the door, smiling.

"It was fine, Mom. I'm not feeling great, though, so I'm going to head up to my room."

"Oh no, are you coming down with something? Mrs. Jenkins across the street had an awful stomach flu last week. Something is going around." She came over and started fussing.

"I'm sure it's nothing," I said, brushing her off. "I'm just tired."

"Go on up, sweetheart. I'll bring you some tea."

"I'm good, but thanks, Mom." I just wanted to be left alone.

"Oh, okay." Dejection coated her words, and I felt like a total bitch. She only cared, and after Dalton, I had to give her that much.

"Honestly, Mom. I'm fine. Nothing a little nap won't solve. Maybe we can watch a movie tonight, the three of us?"

Her smile lifted. "Oh, that would be wonderful. Just like old times. Get some rest, Dayna. I'll make your favorite for dinner."

"Sounds great."

My cell phone burned a hole in my pocket as I headed upstairs. Josh was acting strange. It had only been a couple of days since he left, but it might as well have been weeks. He was too busy to take my calls. Too busy to text me back more than one or two words at a time. Too busy to even tell me he missed me, apparently. And then, when I'd called him out on it, he'd had the audacity to act like *I* was overreacting.

Inside my bedroom, I lay on my bed and pulled out my phone, rereading Josh's most recent text message.

> Josh: God, babe, I'm sorry. Things here are so busy, and I'm a little stressed. I shouldn't have taken it out on you. The team is great. I think I'm going to really love it here. A couple of the guys want to take me out tonight, couldn't say no. So rain check on our video call?

I began typing out a reply but deleted it all, hitting call instead. It rang out, eventually going to voicemail. Only this time, I didn't bother to leave a message.

Space.

He wanted space.

And I wasn't going to spend my summer begging him for attention.

> Me: Have fun. xo

Simple. To the point. Supportive.

I hit send and tucked my phone under my pillow, but it bleeped with an incoming message.

Hope bloomed inside me but dashed when I saw Carson's name, not Josh's.

> Carson: How was your day? Did Aiden behave?

Aiden.

Ugh.

The less said about him, the better.

He'd been okay for most of the day until he started prying about Josh. Asking questions he had no right to ask.

> Me: It was fine. How was your day?

> Carson: Fine? Come on, Bug, give me something. Do I need to kick his ass?

Now that, I'd pay to see. I fought a smile.

> Me: No ass kicking required.

> Carson: I was thinking of taking him out on the boat the day after next, you up for it?

> Me: Do I have to?

> Carson: If I have to go, so do you. Besides, I need my first mate.

I rolled my eyes at that.

> Carson: Come on, Bug. For old time's sake.

> Me: Fine. I'll think about it.

It was only the beginning of the summer break; I couldn't avoid him—or Aiden. But I didn't want to keep answering questions about Josh either. Not when I didn't understand what was going on.

I'd been ready to be with him, to show him that I wanted to make it work. At least, I'd thought I had. But maybe it was a rash decision, trying to hold on to what felt safe and familiar. Because perhaps part of me knew once he left Dupont Beach, our relationship would flounder and part of me wasn't ready for that.

I guess in some ways, I'd taken Josh for granted. He was kind and patient, and committed. Or at least, he had been in Boston. He'd been everything I'd needed. But now everything was different, and I didn't know how to feel about that.

Leaning over, I plucked the small photo frame off the nightstand and ran my finger over Dalton's face. He was in his old high school hockey jersey; his arm slung over my shoulder as we laughed at the camera. I could remember it like it was yesterday—his senior year at high school. He had the whole world at his feet. College. His dreams of going pro. And I was his number one fan.

"God, I miss you, big brother."

He'd have something witty and wise to say about my situation with Josh, no doubt.

Grief splintered inside me, leaving me hollow. But it wasn't only grief. It was knowing that my brother wouldn't have allowed me to wallow. To lie here full of self-doubt and pity, wondering what was wrong with me that my boyfriend didn't want to have sex with me —knowing that it probably had something to do with all the hesitation.

The problem wasn't Josh.

It was me.

And that was the kicker. I'd given him the cold shoulder one too many times, keeping him close but never close enough. I'd taken him for granted, and then, when he'd pulled away, I'd tried to hold on using the only way I knew how—with sex.

It was all my fault we were here now, almost one hundred miles between us, not knowing where I stood.

I'd wanted to wait, to know with absolute certainty that he was the one before I slept with him. But maybe it wasn't that at all. Maybe I'd kept him at arm's length to protect myself. Because if I gave him all of me—if I went all in—and then he left me, I wasn't sure I'd survive it.

Because I'd already lost Dalton.

"Oh, Dalt." I blinked away the tears and closed my eyes, clutching the photo.

I'd loved my big brother more than anything in the world, and he'd left me.

He'd broken my heart.

And it had never healed quite right.

Maybe it never would.

After my self-pity party, I slept like the dead. I didn't even make dinner. So it was no wonder I woke the next morning starving.

Mom cooked up a feast: Pancakes, bacon, eggs, granola, and fruit.

"Whoa, Mom. This is a lot for—" The doorbell rang, and I glanced over my shoulder. "Expecting someone?"

"I invited Aiden. That must be him."

"What?" I balked, eyes widening with horror as I realized the state I was in—tatty-worn pajamas, messy topknot, and weary, tired eyes.

Why does it matter what you look like?

With an inward groan, I dropped my head onto my forearm.

"You look perfectly fine, sweetheart," Mom chuckled.

"What is that supposed to mean?" My head snapped up, and she gave me a knowing smile. "I have a boyfriend," I reminded her.

"Yes, and how is Josh getting on in Toledo?"

"Low blow, Mom, low freaking blow," I called after her, but she disappeared down the hall without a care in the world.

Seconds later, the unwelcome sound of her and Aiden's laughter filled the house. "Thanks for the invite, Mrs. Benson."

"Nonsense, sweetie. It's nice to have company. Isn't that right, Dayna Bug?"

"Sure thing, Mom," I gritted out.

"Morning," Aiden said, giving me a small nod.

"Hey."

He took in my morning appearance and smirked.

"What?" I barked as Mom went over to the coffee machine.

"Nothing. You look very—"

"Don't."

"Someone's a ray of sunshine this morning."

"What are you doing here?" I hissed, keeping my voice low.

"Your mom invited me."

"You didn't have to say yes."

It was bad enough they had invited him over for lunch. But breakfast.

It was too damn early for this crap.

"And miss all of this, freckles?" He wagged a finger in my general direction, and I scowled at him.

"Here you go, Aiden." Mom handed him a plate before placing down his coffee. "Dig in."

"Thanks, Mrs. Ben—"

"Judy, call me Judy."

"Thanks, Judy. This beats stale cereal over at Carson's house any day of the week."

"I've been saying for years that place needs a woman's touch. But between the team and helping out with his parents' charter, it doesn't leave much time for dating."

"Mom, seriously?"

"What?" She gave me a coy smile. "Carson is like a son to us. He deserves to find that special someone. What about you, Aiden, any special girls on the scene? I bet the puck bunnies are lining up for a shot with LU's star player." She flashed him a knowing smile, and he practically choked on his pancake.

I smothered a laugh as I watched him half-drain his coffee to wash it down.

"Uh, no. I'm not really looking to settle down."

"I imagine it's hard to find someone who understands what it's like being a professional athlete."

"I guess." He shrugged, barely meeting my eyes.

"Mom, I'm sure Aiden would rather talk about something else," I said.

"I'm just making small talk, Dayna Bug. Our Dalton was one with the ladies. Always had a line of them showing up on the doorstep hoping for their chance to steal his heart. Remember prom, now that was a hoot—"

"Mom..."

"It's okay to remember him, sweetheart." She gave me a sad smile.

"What was he like?" Aiden asked, surprising me.

"Oh, our Dalton was the best. Loyal and kind, he had a sharp sense of humor," she said with emotion brimming in her eyes. "He believed in standing up for what was right and working hard. There isn't a day that goes by when I don't wish things were different. He would have taken you under his wing, sweetie. That's for sure."

Mom gave Aiden another warm smile. "Anyway," she inhaled a sharp breath, "how are the pancakes?"

"Good, they're really good. It's all great, Judy."

"You should come over every morning. It's been a

long time since I had anyone except Derek to cook for."

"I don't want to make a nuisance of myself." Aiden's gaze flicked to mine, a silent question there. But I was too weary to reply.

If he wanted to come over every morning and eat breakfast with my mom and listen to her stories about Dalton, that was his prerogative.

"Derek will be sad he missed you. Maybe tomorrow he can go into work a little later, and you can share some more stories about the team with him."

"Sure, Judy. Sounds good."

Unbelievable.

I glared at him, my eyes burning holes in the side of his face. When he lifted his gaze to mine, something went through me.

It was very unnerving. But then, he unnerved me. He was too arrogant.

Too everything.

He and Mom launched into a conversation about the upcoming hockey season while I absentmindedly scrolled through social media. It wasn't like I was stalking Josh's socials. They were right there.

But the second I clicked on his profile and scrolled down, I instantly regretted it.

Making new friends, the photo caption read. He'd been tagged in it last night by some girl. I assumed she was the one with her hands all over him. They were both laughing, their attention on each other, not the camera, as if they were sharing a private joke.

"Dayna Bug, what is it? What's wrong?"

"I..." Hurt spread through me as I tried to vocalize what I was feeling. "J-Josh, he—" I couldn't say it. Couldn't bear the thought of people knowing that Josh liked to get up close and personal with girls who were not his girlfriend.

"Sweetheart?"

Aiden frowned; leaning over the breakfast counter, he snatched my phone out of my hand and studied the screen.

"Hey," I protested, embarrassment flooding my cheeks.

"What a douchebag." He slid my cell back across the counter to me. I grabbed it, silently fuming at him.

"Oh, sweetheart." Mom's expression dropped as she leaned over to get a look. "I'm sorry."

"What? It doesn't mean anything." The words caught on the lump in my throat. "She could be his work colleague or his roommate's girlfriend. She could be anyone."

They both stared at me, a mix of pity and sympathy swirling in their eyes.

"He doesn't deserve you, Dayna Bug."

"Come on, Mom," I tried to laugh it off. "It's one photo." I looked down at my phone, only to realize it wasn't one photo. It was a whole album of them.

"Your mom is right," Aiden said. "He doesn't deserve you."

The intensity in his gaze seared me to the bone. I glanced away first, too disarmed by the way he looked at me. I wasn't interesting or puck-bunny beautiful. I was as plain-Jane, average as they came.

Yet when he looked at me, I felt it.

For those few brief seconds, I knew what it felt like to be the center of somebody's world.

But Aiden Dumfries was the bad boy of college hockey. He didn't date. He didn't have a different girl-friend every week. He had conquests—endless notches on his bedposts.

Something I had no intention of ever becoming.

CHAPTER 8

DAYNA

> Josh: I can explain.

> Josh: I know it looks bad, but it isn't what you think. Ellie is a friend of a friend. She was just… Look, Dayna, it was nothing. I promise.

> Josh: I love you. You. Call me and we can talk about it. xo

But I didn't call. I didn't know what to say. He'd said we needed space to figure out what we both wanted, and three days later, there were photos of another woman all over him.

Even if I was overreacting, even if it was innocent, it still hurt. Because Josh was living his life… without me. He hadn't gone to Toledo and mourned our relationship or the distance between us. He'd embraced his new life and thrown himself right into it.

While you were kissing arrogant, cocky hockey players.

Except I hadn't kissed Aiden. He'd kissed me. Not that it really mattered, I supposed.

God, I was a hypocrite and a coward.

But I was confused and scared, and if I was being entirely honest with myself, I was lonely. Being back in Dupont Beach was great. Mom and Dad were great. Seeing Carson again was great. But I had no friends here. I had nothing but memories and heartache.

It was home, though, and I needed to be here. I should have been here long before now. I couldn't explain it, but it was the right decision. I knew that deep down in my heart.

With a heavy sigh, I got up and scanned my room. I needed to do something. Spotting my old running shoes, I slipped them on and headed downstairs.

"Dayna Bug, is that you?"

"Yeah, I'm going for a run."

"A run?" Mom called. "It's late. I'm not sure—"

"I'm a big girl, Mom. I'll be fine. I have my phone with me."

She appeared around the door with a weak smile. "You've been avoiding me."

"No, I just... didn't feel well."

Which is what I'd told her and Aiden after I'd seen the photos of Josh and *Ellie*. Ugh.

"You know, talking about it might help."

"I'm good, I promise. I need some fresh air, though."

"Okay. I'm going to make fish tacos for dinner, so don't be too long."

"Sure thing, Mom." Grabbing a bottle of water from the refrigerator, I headed out into the dusky night, stuffed my earbuds into my ears, and hit play on my favorite playlist.

I hadn't done this in years. Dalton and I used to run together. He was always faster, but he never let me fall behind. When I'd moved to Boston for college, I'd joined the gym and used the treadmill instead. It wasn't the same, but running had always been our thing, and doing it without him just didn't feel right.

But Dalton was gone, and tonight, I really needed to burn off some excess energy.

My feet hit the ground, and the music pulsed through me as I took the path, skirting the edge of the beach. The lake always looked stunning at this time of day, but I kept my eyes ahead, focusing on my breathing. Every single inhale and exhale, the rise and fall of my chest as my feet pounded against the asphalt.

When I reached the end of the path, I looped back around, but this time, I cut on the beach and ran along the shore, slowing my pace a little to allow myself time to catch my breath. My lungs burned, muscles I hadn't used in forever pinging with exertion. But I felt good.

For the first time in a really long time, I felt free.

A figure up ahead caught my eye, and I slowed to a complete stop, watching in awe as Aiden waded out of the lake in dark board shorts that hugged his hips. My heart fluttered wildly in my chest. I'd seen him half-naked already, but I hadn't seen him like this. Drenched in water, his hair wet and mussed up, every dip and plane of his body glistening under the moon-light. His body was a work of art.

He was—

Staring. Right. At. Me.

Crap.

Heat flooded my cheeks as he made his way toward me.

"Don't you know it's rude to stare," he said.

"You're on my beach."

"Your beach, huh?" The faintest of smiles traced his mouth. "Bit late for a run, isn't it?"

"How did you know?"

"The sweaty, flushed, breathless mess gave you

away. Although I guess you could have been doing something else."

"Oh my God, you can't say that," I murmured under my breath, running a hand over my hair.

"Relax, I'm joking. You look... nice pants."

I glanced down at my yoga pants and internally cursed—first pajamas and now skintight yoga pants.

When I looked back up, he was still staring at my legs. "Eyes up here, hotshot." I clicked my fingers, and he blinked.

"You done hiding, or should I expect you to disappear into thin air any second?"

"I wasn't—" I pressed my lips together, swallowing my argument. Because he was right, I had spent the day hiding, licking my wounds.

"What did you do all day?" I changed the subject.

"A bit of this and a bit of that."

"Are you always like this?" My brow arched.

"Charming? Funny? Mysterious?"

"I was going to go with an ass, but whatever."

"Did you talk to the boyfriend?"

"That's none of your business."

Aiden held up his hands. "I'm not trying to be a dick, freckles. I just thought maybe you'd want to talk."

"Why on earth would I talk to you about my

boyfriend troubles? And for the love of God, please stop calling me that."

"Ah, so there is trouble in paradise."

"You saw the photos."

And I hated that he had. It was one of the reasons I'd fled to my room, feigning a stomachache.

"She was hot."

"Geez, way to make a girl feel better about herself."

"That's not... fuck." He ran a hand down his face. "That was a shitty thing to say, sorry."

"Why'd you say it then?"

"Because I'm an ass, freckles."

I smiled. I couldn't help it.

"Want to sit?" He motioned to his pile of stuff.

"I guess."

We sat down, and I was hyper-aware of how close he was, like the other night when he'd kissed me.

"Don't worry, I won't do it again," he quietly said as if he could hear my thoughts.

"How did you— actually, don't answer that."

"So the boyfriend... Did you talk to him? Get his side of the story?"

"Not really. He keeps texting me."

"Let me guess. It's nothing?" He peeked up at me. "She's a friend. It's not what you think?"

"That's—" I stopped myself. Because he was

right, that was exactly it. "The night before he left...
He said he thought some space would be a good
thing."

"Ouch."

"Right? I mean, I know I'm not the easiest girl in
the world to love."

"What?" He reared back a little.

"I guess I've been keeping him at arm's length. We
haven't... you know." Aiden gawked at me as if I was
talking in another language, and I added, "Sex. We
haven't had sex yet."

"But your mom said you've been dating for almost
nine months."

"My mom has a big mouth, but she's right. We
have."

"And you haven't had sex."

"Correct."

God, why had I told him? But it was out now. And
strangely, I didn't mind.

"How is that even possible?"

"I guess you would say that," I murmured, rolling
my eyes as I stared out at the lake.

"Whoa, what the fuck is that supposed to mean?"

"I've heard the stories, Aiden."

"Right." He tensed. "Because the stories are always
true. I'm the bad boy of the Lakeshore U Lakers.

Fighting and fucking my way through college. I'm glad we cleared that up."

I winced at the anger in his words, the pain. "Sorry, I didn't mean—"

"Yeah." He looked over at me. "You did."

"Well, it was a shitty thing to say."

"Yeah, it was."

"Guess that makes us even." I smiled.

Something crackled between us. The same spark that had existed that first night. I wasn't a huge believer in fate or destiny or kismet. How could I be when I'd lost my brother. But I felt it now like I had that night.

"Have you ever been surrounded by people only to feel totally alone?" he asked, his voice a quiet, uncertain whisper on the breeze.

"All the time."

"Sometimes we do stupid shit to feel something, Dayna. To remind us that we're alive."

His words hit me like bullets, tearing through my carefully constructed defenses. Whatever pain, betrayal, and heartache Aiden had lived through, it had deeply affected him.

I saw that now.

He was lost. Fighting to survive was the only way he knew how.

"You're not your father, you know," I said, immediately regretting the words. I didn't know Aiden, not really. Not well enough to pass comment on his father or their relationship. But sometimes, people needed to hear the truth.

They needed someone to offer them a life raft.

Josh had been that person for me once. Maybe I could be that person for Aiden.

"It doesn't matter." His eyes bore into mine. "I'll always be Dawson Dumfries' kid; no matter what I do, what I achieve, I'll never escape his shadow."

"Only you get to define your future, Aiden."

"Is that so? And what about your future, Dayna?"

"What do you mean?"

"Why haven't you had sex with your boyfriend?"

"I..." Heat rose up inside me. "We are not talking about me."

"Why?"

"Because it's different." My chest tightened. "I'm not..."

"Cat got your tongue, freckles?" He smirked, and I wanted to wipe it off his ridiculously gorgeous face.

The devil in sheep's clothing.

That's who Aiden Dumfries was.

And he was so, so dangerous for a girl like me. For my fragile, weary heart.

"I need to go," I said, clambering to my feet. But Aiden caught my wrist, holding me there.

"Don't you want to know what I think?"

"No, I really, really don't," I snarled. Hating the way he made me feel. The way my heart raced in my chest, wild and untamed. How my skin burned right where he touched me.

It had never felt this way with Josh.

Ever.

If being with Josh was like riding the Ferris Wheel, being around Aiden was like being on the pendulum ride, my heart crashing in my chest, waiting for the next rush.

"I'm going to tell you anyway. Maybe..." He leaned up close, his warm breath fanning my face. "Maybe deep down, you know he isn't good enough for you."

Yanking my arm free, I stumbled back, glaring at him. "You don't know anything about Josh and me, and I'd prefer to keep it that way."

But as I hurried away from him, my stomach a tight ball of nerves, I realized that maybe Aiden Dumfries knew more than I wanted to admit.

CHAPTER 9

AIDEN

"You're extra broody this morning," Carson said, offering me a fresh mug of coffee.

"Thanks." I took it, ignoring his observation.

I was... pissed? Frustrated? Oddly intrigued by a girl I had no right thinking about.

But I couldn't stop myself. Dayna Benson consumed my thoughts; she'd even wormed her way into my fucking dreams. I'd woken in a ball of sweat, my dick rock hard and aching, as hazy memories of her naked body pressed up against mine flickered through my mind.

"Have you talked to Dayna?" I asked.

Fuck. Why did I ask that?

"Dayna? Only to arrange the boat trip later. Why?"

"Nothing." I nursed my coffee, wondering when things had gotten so complicated.

I didn't do complicated—my life was already enough of a shit show to add in girl drama. It's why I didn't date. Why the second a girl got too clingy—usually after one night, two if she was lucky—I cut her loose.

"What aren't you telling me?" Carson pushed, and I lifted my gaze to his, frowning.

"Her boyfriend got caught in some photos on social media."

"What kind of photos?" A flash of irritation coasted over his expression.

"Could be something. Could be nothing. My money says he's dicking around on her."

"Shit. You think he's cheating on her? He's barely been gone a week."

"Looked pretty up close and personal with some girl in the photos. Dayna was upset and spent the day avoiding everyone."

"She talked to you about this?" His brow lifted.

"I went for a late-night swim. She was jogging on the beach. We talked a little."

I left out the part where I'd overstepped, and she'd stormed off again.

"What did she say?"

"Did you know they haven't... you know."

"Seriously, you're talking to me about her sex life?" Carson blanched. "She's like a fucking sister to me."

"You don't think it's weird they haven't—"

"I swear to God, Aiden."

"Geez, relax. It's just sex."

He blew out a steady breath, the muscle in his jaw clenching. "They really haven't..."

"Nope. Weird, right?"

"I mean, I'm sure she has her reasons. But they've been dating for eight months. I just assumed..."

"Well, the asshole seems to be having no problem with the ladies up in Toledo."

"You like her?" Carson pinned me with a hard look.

"Who, Dayna? I mean, she's okay." I shrugged. "As far as girls go. But I don't—"

"You should see your face right now."

"Fuck off."

"Real mature, Dumfries. I appreciate you looking out for her, I do, but the last thing she needs is to rebound with a guy like you." I bristled, and he added, "Chill. I don't mean it as the personal attack you're thinking. But you're... you. I haven't known you to be around the same girl for more than a night in the time I've known you."

"I could say the same thing about you, *Coach*."

"Good thing we're not talking about me, then." He shook his head, but I saw the amusement in his eyes. "Dayna is important to me, and she's been through a lot. I'm going to ask you this once and only once. Do I need to be worried here?"

"Relax, I'm not looking for a summer hookup." And if I were, I sure as hell wouldn't pick a girl like Dayna.

"Good because she's worth more than that."

"I just don't like seeing her get taken for a fool."

"Well, fuck me, Dumfries. Who knew you had a heart underneath all that brooding grumpy exterior?"

I flipped him off, and he chuckled. But his smile dropped, giving away to concern. "You really think he's messing around behind her back?"

"A twenty-two-year-old guy who hasn't had sex in at least eight months suddenly living it up in the city after he told his girlfriend he thought some space would be a good idea ... I know what I'd be doing if I were him." My brow went up, and Carson scrubbed his jaw.

"Fuck, he said that?" I nodded, and he cursed

under his breath, adding, "I knew there was something off about him."

"The question is what—"

The doorbell pierced the air, and Carson frowned. "I wonder who that is."

But my gut told me who he'd find standing on the doorstep, so I was hardly surprised when Dayna trailed into the kitchen behind him, carrying what looked like a picnic basket.

"I figured we could get an early start." She gave me a weak smile. "I also brought you these."

"Let me guess," I said, taking the container from her. "Apology muffins?"

"Something like that."

"Does someone want to explain to me what's going on?" Carson cocked a brow at me.

"Ask Dayna."

"I... I was a bitch. It seems Aiden brings that side out in me." Her mouth twitched, and I had the sudden urge to kiss her again.

Jesus. What the fuck was wrong with me?

She was just a girl.

She had a boyfriend, even if he was a cheating asshole. Not to mention a shit ton of emotional baggage and intimacy issues.

She had apology muffins, for fuck's sake.

"Can I trust the two of you not to try and kill each other on The Deke?"

"The Deke? What the fuck is The Deke?"

Dayna laughed, the sound fisting my heart to the point of pain.

I needed to get a fucking grip.

"The Deke is Carson's pride and joy. Isn't that right, Cars?"

"Damn right it is."

"Seriously, you called your boat The Deke?" I asked, draining my coffee.

"Which is exactly what I said," Dayna smiled.

"The Deke is a good fucking name. I thought you, of all people, would appreciate it," Carson grumbled. "I'm going to grab my things. Will you two be okay for a minute?"

"I think we can manage," Dayna said.

"And you"—he leveled me with a knowing look—"behave."

The second Carson was gone, she looked at me and frowned. "What did he mean, behave?"

Oh fuck.

"Nothing," I replied.

She snatched the container off the counter and flipped the lid, helping herself to a muffin. "You, Aiden Dumfries, are a terrible liar."

If only she knew how right she was.

Thanks to Dayna, I knew that The Deke was a twenty-foot bowrider that Carson and Dalton had fully restored with Carson's dad when they were both young boys.

I wasn't a boat guy. I was an ice and hockey guy. I preferred keeping my feet flat on the ground—or skates as the case usually was. But there was something pretty awesome about racing across Lake Erie on Carson's boat.

The spray was refreshing, cooling us off in the midmorning heat. Within minutes of getting out on the water, Dayna had slipped off her t-shirt to reveal a plain black bikini top that may as well have been silk and lace for how fucking hot she looked in the damn thing.

I was having a really hard time not staring at her curves. So much so that I had no choice but to turn my back on her.

"So, what do you think?" Carson grinned as he eased his hand off the throttle, and The Deke began to slow. We were at least a mile out from shore.

"I can see the appeal," I said.

"See Cedar Point over there?" He pointed to the distance. "And in that direction is Kelley's Island. Another beer?" he asked, leaning back to rummage in the cooler.

"Sure."

"Bug, you want a soda?"

"I'm good," she said, catching my eye.

I smiled, but she barely smiled back. I guess I deserved that. I had shunned her for most of the morning. But I couldn't look at her in that fucking bikini top without wanting to tear it off her body, preferably with my teeth.

"You good?" Carson asked, handing me a beer. "You seem tense."

"Nope, I'm fine."

"Fine, right." The fucker smirked.

He knew.

Of course, he fucking knew, and I didn't doubt that once we made it back to shore, he'd give me shit for it. Reminding me that Dayna was off-limits.

"Do you think you can take the helm while I go talk to her?"

"You want me to drive the boat?" I gawked at him.

"It's hardly rocket science. Just keep her steady."

"Sure, I can handle it."

"Didn't doubt it for a second, hotshot." He chuckled, climbing around to get to the front of the boat. "Hey," he said, sitting down beside her.

"Hey."

The compact design didn't afford them any privacy, so I could hear every word.

"Penny for your thoughts?"

"I told Josh I think we should end things."

My hands tightened around the wheel, the blood draining from my knuckles.

"You did?"

"Yeah. It's not going to work." She gave Carson a sad smile. "Me here, him there. And I keep thinking... maybe there's a reason I kept him at a distance, you know?"

"You deserve someone who will put you first, Dayna."

"I know that, I do. But honestly, I'm not even sure what that means. I've spent so long hiding, Cars."

He wrapped an arm around her shoulder, and she rested her head on his chest. Jealousy surged inside of me, a feeling I was really fucking unfamiliar with.

I barely knew her.

It made no fucking sense.

But it didn't seem to matter. Because watching

them together, I wanted it to be me. I wanted to be the one comforting her.

And that was a huge fucking problem.

We sailed on the lake for another couple of hours. Carson's love of the water and his precious boat bled from every word, every smile, and laugh. Dayna joined us, too, putting on a brave face as we zipped up and down the lake.

By the time we reached the dock, my skin felt crispy, and I was fucking starving despite the lunch Mrs. Benson had packed us.

"You two up for a pizza and a fire?" Carson asked as he and Dayna moored the boat.

"Sounds good." She gave him a smile and then slid her gaze to mine.

"Sure," I said, not entirely certain if I was answering him or the silent question in her eyes.

Her mood swings were giving me whiplash.

We all piled into Carson's truck and drove the short distance back to his house. "Do you want to invite your parents?" he asked Dayna.

"Is it awful if I say no?"

He chuckled, "Of course not, Bug."

"We could always go to a bar and get shitfaced," I suggested out of nowhere.

"I don't think that's—"

"Actually, I think that sounds like a great idea," Dayna grinned.

"You do?" Carson frowned.

"We could go to Moonies and order some dirty fries and some pitchers of beer."

"You want to eat dirty fries and drink beer at Moonies?" He looked at her like she'd lost her mind.

"What the fuck is a Moonies?" I asked.

"It's a dive bar in Dupont Beach."

"You and Dalton used to love sneaking into that dive bar, if I remember correctly."

"Dirty fries and beer sound like my kind of place," I said. "I'm in."

"I knew I could count on you, hotshot."

It was a dig. Her attempt at getting under my skin. And fuck me if it wasn't working.

"This is a bad idea," Carson said, pulling that older brother-responsible coach routine he loved so much.

I clapped him on the back and smirked, still holding Dayna's gaze.

"Bad ideas are the best kind."

CHAPTER 10

AIDEN

"What did I tell you?" Carson murmured, tipping his beer in the direction where Dayna was laughing with a couple of older women. "This was a bad fucking idea."

"Relax, she's just cutting loose."

"Are you going to hold her hair later when her dirty fries make a reappearance?"

"Maybe I will."

"Over my dead fucking body." He glowered at me.

"Chill, I'm joking." Mostly.

The truth was, I liked Dayna like this. Goofy and drunk. She wasn't wasted, but she had a nice buzz thanks to all the liquor she'd drank since we arrived at Moonies.

"Whew." She flounced over and flopped down beside me. "I need a drink."

"Water." Carson shoved a bottle toward her. "You need water."

"Carson Bear Walsh, I am—"

"Hold up, Bear? Your middle name is *Bear*?"

"You didn't know?" Dayna grinned.

"No, no, I did not," I smirked at Carson, and he flipped me off.

"If you say anything to the rest of the team, I'll—"

"You'll what, Coach? Bench me? You don't have that kind of power."

"No, but I can make you skate drills until your legs fall off."

"Oh my God." Dayna slammed her palms down on the table, making our drinks rattle. "I love this song. Come on, Cars, dance with me."

"Oh no, Bug. You're on your own with this one."

"But you have to dance with me. My boyfriend —*ex*-boyfriend—is a cheating asshole, and I'm cele-brating my newfound freedom. It's my breakup party. There has to be dancing. Hotshot"—she pinned me with a serious look, fisting her hands on her hips —"you too, let's go."

"I don't dance."

Her brows furrowed, and she looked so fucking cute. "No, you just kiss girls without their—"

Thankfully Dayna's new friends intercepted her, dragging her off to the small dance floor in the corner of the bar.

"What did she just say?" Carson glared at me.

"No idea. Sounded like a drunken ramble if you ask me." I sipped my beer, glancing to the dance floor. Dayna was dancing with her arms thrown high in the air, a wide smile painted on her face. But I saw the shadows in her eyes. Josh had done a real number on her.

"I could drive to Toledo and wring his fucking neck," Carson murmured.

Want backup? I wanted to ask but swallowed the words.

Jesus.

What was it about this girl that had gotten under my skin?

I wanted to hate it, and part of me did, but I also found myself anticipating her next snarky comment, another exasperated smile, any scraps of attention she'd throw my way.

"What?" Carson asked me, and I shook my head.

"Nothing."

"You're not fooling anyone," he said cryptically.

"I have no idea what you're talking about."

"Hmm, we'll see." He wrapped his fingers on the table, standing. "I'm going to get another beer. You want anything?"

My gaze flicked to the dance floor again, to Dayna, and back to him.

"No, I'm good."

Liar.

But the one thing I wanted was so far out of my reach that all I could do was watch.

"She's like the Energizer Bunny on crack," Carson said sometime later.

My brows went up, a smirk playing on my lips, and he balked.

"Fuck, I did not mean... get your mind out of the gutter. It's been an hour, and she's still going."

"She needs this," I said.

I knew what it was like to reach for a distraction—something to numb the pain inside. Hockey, college parties, girls... It was the perfect recipe for an escape.

One I'd spent the better part of three years overindulging in.

At Lakeshore U, I was somebody. I was the Lakers' star player, but that was it. Nobody knew Aiden Dumfries, the guy who had grown up in the shadow of his piece of shit father.

I'd worked my ass off to shake the stain he'd left on my childhood, but I would never fully escape it. So yeah, I knew what it was like to want to escape, to want to be someone else—just for a little while.

Carson's phone started ringing, and he frowned at the screen as he snatched it up. "Mom, what is— yeah, calm down. I'll be there. No, no, it's fine. I can walk— yeah."

"Problem?" I asked as he hung up.

"My old man hurt himself trying to rig the boat. I told the stubborn old fool to wait until the morning."

"You want me to come—"

"No, stay here. Keep an eye on Dayna. She deserves this, just... just don't let her drink anything else, okay?"

I nodded, a strange sensation rippling through me.

Carson stood and shoved his cell in his jeans pocket. "I don't need to remind you, but she's—"

"Off-limits. I got the memo, Coach. I am capable of keeping my hands to myself, you know."

His expression flickered with doubt. "Just remember, Dumfries, there will be a lot of drills in your future if you fuck her over."

"I'm not—"

"Hey." Dayna appeared, her skin glowing, her eyes slightly glazed, and her voice a little breathless. "What's going on?" She glanced between us, concern pinching her brows.

"I've got to take off, but Aiden is going to stick around to make sure you get home okay."

"Cars, I'm a grown woman. I can take care—"

"Aiden is going to stick around." He hooked his arm around her neck and dropped a kiss on her head. "Try to behave. I'll call you tomorrow."

"Say hi to your folks for me," she shouted to him as he walked off.

"How did you know it was his folks?" I asked.

"Because I know Carson." She smiled fondly, sliding into the booth opposite of me. "I need a drink." I arched a brow, and she chuckled, "Water, *Dad*."

"Are you having fun?"

"I'd be having more fun if you or Carson danced with me." She batted her eyelashes, all sweet and sexy and pure fucking temptation.

Jesus, what had I gotten myself into?

"Already told you, freckles, I don't dance."

"You don't dance. You don't date. What *does* a guy like you do?"

"I'm not sure you want to know the answer to that."

Her eyes flared with interest. But she was drunk. And I wasn't looking to be her rebound, no matter how fucking adorable she looked, gazing at me with that pouty mouth of hers.

"Dayna, you need to stop looking at me like that," I growled.

"W-what? How am I looking at you?"

This was dangerous territory. But I couldn't help myself; I couldn't resist her allure. She was so different from the puck bunnies at Lakeshore U.

"Aiden?" she whispered, still staring at me. Gazing at me with those big doe-eyes.

"You should drink this." I shoved the bottle of water toward her.

Her expression guttered, the heat that had been building between us blinking out. "Okay."

"Do you want to talk about it?" I asked.

"About what?"

"Josh."

"I... He says nothing happened with her, but he's lying."

"How can you be so sure?"

She gave a small shrug, focusing on the bottle in

her hands. "I just know. I kept him at arm's length, and, in the end, I pushed him into another girl's arms. He's twenty-two, and I made him wait all this time, and, in the end, he realized I wasn't worth it."

"Hey, don't make excuses for him."

My hand curled into a fist against my thigh. I was an asshole. I rarely fucked the same girl twice, but I never made promises. They knew what they were getting, and if they expected more, that was on them.

But Josh had made promises to Dayna. He'd stood by her side for months. *Months.* And at the first taste of freedom, he'd fucked her over.

"Can I ask you something?"

Dayna nodded.

"Why'd you two never... you know?"

"Dalton's death broke me. It broke me in ways I didn't think were possible. I was so lost, Aiden. It's why I stayed away, why I..."

"Hey, you don't have to tell me. I shouldn't have—"

"No"—she forced a smile—"it's okay. I think it's time I talked about it."

She drained half the bottle of water and wiped her mouth with the back of her hand. "I closed myself off after my brother's death. Carson tried. He tried so hard to help me heal, but, in the end, I needed to get away from Dupont Beach. College was hard at first. I found it difficult to make friends, to let people in.

"Cancer, right?"

She nodded, pain glittering in her eyes.

I'd heard the story—everyone at Lakeshore U had.

Dalton Benson and Carson Walsh were an urban myth around campus—a legend. Best friends who rose through the ranks together right out of peewee. The dynamic duo. Two of college hockey's rising stars, both playing for the Lakers.

Until Dalton got sick at the end of freshman year.

"It came out of nowhere," her voice cracked. "And within four months, he was gone. It didn't feel real. One day he was there, still laughing in his hospital bed, cussing at the TV whenever we watched the Blue Jackets play. And then he was gone."

"I'm sorry."

"Thanks. I can talk about it now, but it took me a long time to come to terms with it. Part of me never will. He was my big brother, you know. The person I looked up to more than anything. And he was going places, Aiden. He was going all the way."

"He still holds the record for most goals scored by a right-winger at Lakeshore," I said. I only knew because Noah, our star right-winger, had made it his mission to try and beat it.

"I know. I check the end-of-season stats every year."

Sadness radiated from her, and I wanted to fix it. For the first time ever, I wanted to put the sparkle back in a girl's eyes and make her smile again.

Fuck.

She obviously had some kind of magical powers because she was doing things to me no other girl ever had.

"It was too hard being here, being reminded of him every second of every day. So I moved to Boston and never looked back.

"I didn't officially meet Josh until last summer. We had some mutual friends, and we'd seen each other around, but I didn't put myself out there."

"What changed?"

"I was tired of being lonely, and Josh, he made things better. He was kind, patient, and driven. But I don't know. There was never that spark. That inexplicable attraction."

"He was safe," I said, and she nodded. "Do you love him?"

"I— I think so, just not the way I'm supposed to. Does that make me a horrible person?"

"You can't force these things," I said. Like I was a

qualified expert in these matters. The only person I'd ever loved was my mom.

"But something must be wrong with me, right? I mean, Josh is perfect. On paper he's perfect, but I..." Tears pricked the corner of her eyes, and I wanted nothing more than to pull Dayna into my arms and comfort her.

What the fuck?

"Oh, I don't know what I'm saying," she sniffled. "I'm drunk, and it's late. We should probably go."

"Whatever you want," I said, draining the last of my beer. Dayna watched me intently, and I asked, "What?"

"I was wrong, Aiden Dumfries. You are nothing like they say you are."

"Don't be fooled, freckles. I'm not the good guy here."

I didn't know how to be. Yet, sitting here, listening to her story, the pain in her voice, it made me wish I was.

"Come on, let's get you home." I stood and offered her my hand. The second her palm slid against mine, a shiver ran down my spine.

Fuck me.

This girl.

This fucking girl.

It was because Carson had marked her as off-limits. Guys were wired to want the chase—the hunt. Being told I couldn't have her was like laying a challenge at my feet.

And I never backed down from a challenge.

But something about this—about her—felt different.

We walked out of Moonies in a thick silence. Dayna swayed gently on her feet, humming a tune as we walked toward the beach.

"We can get a cab," I suggested.

"No, I like the walk. Besides, I should probably give myself some time to sober up before I get home and Mom starts fussing."

"She'll wait up?"

Dayna chuckled. "You've met Judy Benson. Of course, she'll wait up."

We were still holding hands, but Dayna didn't seem to mind. Besides, it wasn't like I could let go of her. She'd probably face-plant on the sidewalk.

"She seems like a good mom."

"She is. The best." Dayna grinned. "But after Dalton... I'm surprised she let me go to Boston."

"It must have been hard on her and your dad."

She nodded. "But I needed space. I needed to find myself again."

"Did you?"

"Did I what?" She peeked up at me.

"Find yourself."

"Honestly?" Pain shone in her eyes as she gave me a weak smile. "I'm not sure."

CHAPTER 11

DAYNA

"Come on, let's walk across the beach," I said, needing to stop Aiden from looking at me like that.

He was so different from Josh. I couldn't really put my finger on it, but he was just... more. He had the kind of eyes that pierced you, made you melt with the intensity in his gaze, leaving your heart fluttering wildly in your chest. Even when utter crap was spewing out of his mouth, his eyes were captivating.

It wasn't any wonder he had hordes of girls falling over themselves at Lakeshore U. Aiden had that charm about him. The cocky bad boy that girls wanted to tame. But there was something wild in his gaze. Something I knew would never be conquered.

He followed me as I took off toward the water's edge. I bent down to slip off my sandals and dig my feet into the sand, loving how the fine grains felt against my skin.

"Want to go skinny dipping?" His words danced over my shoulder, making a shudder roll down my spine as he stepped up behind me.

"I think Carson would have something to say about that."

"Don't you ever just want to live in the moment? Say to hell with the rules and people's expectations of what you should do?"

I looked up at him, our mouths so close that if I leaned up a fraction, I'd be kissing him.

Kissing him.

God, that wasn't supposed to sound so appealing, yet I couldn't think about anything else.

"Freckles?" he breathed, and I swallowed, forcing myself to take a step away—to put some distance between us. Aiden chuckled, "Do I make you nervous?"

"A little."

"That's cute."

"Cute?" I groaned. "You make me sound like a thirteen-year-old girl with braids and a retainer."

His eyes dropped down my body and back up

again. "Trust me, that is not what I'm thinking right now."

"What are you thinking?" I asked, a little breathless. Because the way he looked at me... no one had ever looked at me like that before.

Not even Josh.

Especially not Josh.

"Nothing good." The words tumbled through me.

"Kiss me," I blurted out.

"Dayna..." His eyes shuttered. When they opened again, all the heat was gone from them. "You know we can't."

"Can't?" I stepped closer, craning my neck to look at him. "Or won't? I'm not *that* drunk if that's what you're worried about. And I won't run off and tell Carson. But I need... I need to know what it feels like." His brows pinched, and I added, "I need to know what it feels like to live in the moment."

Because I realized now that I never allowed myself to truly let go. Josh was safe. He was exactly what I needed at the time when we'd first met. But he didn't push me out of my comfort zone. He let me remain there. Even when it came to sex, he let me standstill. Sure, he occasionally tried to take things further, but something always felt wrong about it.

Maybe because he was wrong for me.

God, I was so confused.

But Carson had said something to me—he'd said that Josh wasn't the kind of guy he pictured me with. He didn't like small-town life or follow hockey or enjoy lazy days at the beach. He liked order and routine and everything in its set place.

"We should go, freckles," Aiden said, jolting me from the memories.

"G-go? You want to go?"

"I want to get you home before I do something very stupid."

"You want to kiss me," I said.

"Thought I'd made that pretty obvious the first time I found you down here."

"So, what's stopping you now?"

"Things are different now." He let out a heavy sigh. "I know you, and I don't want to hurt you."

I scoffed at that. "Because I'm not a puck bunny, right? Because I'm a virgin? I'm not, you know?"

"The fuck?" He gawked at me.

"It's true. I had sex with some guy at a party the summer before I left for college... It was horrible. I hated every second and immediately regretted it. Shit," I clapped a hand over my mouth, "I've never told anyone that before."

"Let me get this straight. You gave it up to some

random guy but wouldn't sleep with your boyfriend of eight months?"

"I know, it sounds bad when you say it like that, but I—"

"Stop." Aiden pressed his finger to my lips. "It's your body, freckles. Your rules. I just... shit, your first time must have been bad since you haven't wanted to do it again."

"I've wanted to do it." The words spilled out of their own volition. "I just didn't want to do it with... Josh."

"I almost feel sorry for the guy."

"It's a mess. I know that. Not that it matters now, we're done. It's over." If I was being one hundred percent honest with myself, it should have been over a while ago.

I gazed up at Aiden, silently willing him to concede. It was one tiny kiss. It didn't have to mean anything.

"It's late. We should—"

"What are you so scared of?" I jabbed my finger at his chest. "I thought you were the infallible Aiden Dumfries."

"Careful, freckles." He snagged my hand, holding it suspended between us. "Play with fire, and you might end up burned."

"I think I can take the heat."

Oh God. What was wrong with me? I was acting like a little hussy. But I had all this restless energy. And I wanted him to kiss me.

I wanted to know what the big deal was.

"It's just one kiss," I said, pushing my hand against his until my fingers grazed his chest.

"Dayna..." He inhaled a sharp breath, torment swirling in his ice-blue eyes.

He wanted to kiss me.

But there were a million reasons why he shouldn't.

A million reasons that seemed inconsequential at that very moment.

"Fine." I went to walk away. "Forget I said any—"

Aiden grabbed and hauled me into his arms, staring down at me like I was both the bane of and the reason for his existence. A thrill went through me, and then he whispered, "Fuck it," before slamming his mouth down on mine.

Sweet baby Jesus, it was a kiss to end all kisses.

A kiss I knew would ruin me for all other kisses.

Aiden's lips moved against mine with perfect finesse. His tongue snaked out, tasting me, teasing the seam of my mouth until I parted my lips and let him in.

"More," I murmured, clutching onto his broad shoulders, practically climbing his body.

Our tongues tangled in soft lazy, licks that had my toes curling into the damp sand, sparks firing off around my body.

Aiden was a little more than a stranger, and he definitely wasn't the kind of guy I needed to get tangled up with. But I couldn't stop myself. Because kissing Aiden, under the moonlight in my favorite place in the entire world, I'd never felt more alive.

"Feel this." I grabbed his hand and pressed it against my chest, right over my heart. "Feel how fast it's beating. You did that."

"Fuck, Dayna."

"What?" I grinned up at him.

"You." He pushed the flyaway hairs out of my face and leaned down, capturing my lips in another bruising kiss.

"Mmm, I like kissing you."

"You're drunk," he said, bopping my nose.

"I am not." His brow arched, and a small giggle bubbled out of me. "Okay, maybe just a little. But I'm sober enough to know what I want."

"Are you sure about that?" His hand glided down my spine and over the curve of my ass.

His touch was possessive and full of promises. But it felt good. Right.

"Aid—"

"We should go," he cut me off, bursting my bubble.

"You can go," I said petulantly. "I'm not ready to leave yet."

"Dayna—"

But I'd already yanked out of his hold and dropped down onto the sand, lying on my back and staring up at the inky night sky. "It's so beautiful," I sighed.

"Yeah," he replied.

But when I looked at him, he wasn't looking at the sky; he was watching me.

"I thought you were leaving."

"You thought wrong." Aiden kicked off his sneakers and sat down beside me.

"I won't tell anyone... about the kiss."

"Good."

A strange sensation went through me. Was he ashamed of me? Or was he just worried about what Carson would say?

Silence enveloped us. A minute ago, things had been flirty and fun, but now things felt strained. Like I'd messed everything up by asking him to kiss me.

I threw an arm over my eyes and let out a heavy sigh.

"Freckles?"

"Why do you call me that?" I lowered my arm, peeking over at him.

Aiden gave me a rare smile and leaned over me, his fingers gently tracing my face. "Because you have the cutest freckles right here." The brush of his fingers over my warm skin made me shudder.

"What's your magic number?"

He made a choking noise, gawking at me like I'd lost my mind. "You do not want to know that."

"Maybe I do."

Maybe it'll remind me we're too different. The bad boy and the good girl trying to overcome her grief.

"You know my number," I said. "It's only fair I get to know yours."

"Dayna, come on, it's not the same." Aiden shifted onto his side, leaning on his fist as he loomed over me.

"More than ten?" He grimaced, and my stomach dipped. "Okay, more than twenty?" I asked.

Aiden visibly flinched, and my brows furrowed. "Fifty?"

"Dayna..."

"More than one hundred?"

"I don't keep a list," he snorted.

"Wow, that's a lot of girls." A strange sensation went through me, plunking in my stomach.

He was so experienced, used to puck bunnies lining up for him, willing to give him whatever he wanted. And I might as well have been a virgin.

"I like sex. I'm always safe, and they know I'm not..."

"Looking for anything serious."

"Yeah." His eyes crinkled. "It is what it is. I won't apologize for who I am."

"I didn't ask you to."

"I've never done this, though."

"What?"

"Lie on a beach under the moonlight with a girl."

"Are you saying I now own one of your firsts, Aiden Dumfries?"

"I'm saying," he inched closer, running his hand along the side of my collarbone and curling it around the back of my neck. "You own two."

"Two?"

He kissed me, shaping my mouth with his lips. It was different from the kiss before. As if he was savoring it, savoring me.

"Yeah," he breathed, touching his head to mine. "I've never kissed a girl on the beach before either."

"Mmm, I like this game." I curled my fist into his t-shirt and yanked him closer.

"This is a bad idea," he warned.

"I know what I'm doing, Aiden."

"Yeah?" He pulled back to look me in the eye. "And what is that?"

"Living in the moment."

And right now, at this very moment, I wanted Aiden Dumfries.

CHAPTER 12

AIDEN

DAYNA BENSON WAS GOING to be the death of me.

She stared at me with those big lust-filled eyes, and my resolve snapped.

I wasn't a good guy. I fucked girls like I scored goals on the ice. I got into more fights than just a little. And I had no plans to settle down. Love was for pussies.

But I wanted Dayna. I'd wanted her ever since the moment I'd laid eyes on her. And here she was offering herself up to me on a silver fucking platter.

"You don't know what you're asking for?" I murmured, fighting the urge to grab her and kiss the shit out of her.

"Yes, I do." She practically purred the words. "One

night. And tomorrow, everything goes back to normal."

Normal.

Why did her words leave me with a sour taste in my mouth?

That's all this could ever be, wasn't it?

Carson had already warned me to stay away from her. If we crossed this line, I was directly betraying his trust.

"Aiden, please." Dayna ran her hand down my chest, going lower until her fingers grazed my dick.

Fuck.

"I want this. I want you." She ran her nose along my jaw, kissing the corner of my mouth. "I want to know what it feels like."

Sex.

She wanted sex.

I wasn't an idiot. I knew she wanted to get back at Josh for hurting her. Usually, I'd have no problem giving a girl what she wanted—especially one as pretty as Dayna.

So why the fuck was I hesitating?

"It'll be our little secret." She pressed her body closer to mine, demanding my full attention. She felt soft against me, and I couldn't resist trailing my hand up the back of her leg and slipping it up inside her skirt.

"That feels good," she whispered, her breath catching as I dragged my finger over her damp panties.

"If you think that feels good, wait until I'm buried deep inside you."

"Yes, that. I want that. I want to feel you."

"One night," I reiterated.

Dayna pressed her lips together, nodding. And then whispered, "Our secret."

I was going to hell.

But I couldn't deny her. Not when I knew how fucking good she tasted. Not when I'd spent all night watching her dance and laugh, imagining what she was hiding under her ridiculously little skirt and sheer blouse.

"Our secret," I whispered against her mouth, flicking my tongue along the seam of her lips.

Dayna pulled me down on top of her, looping her arms around my neck. I nestled between her legs, grinding my hips a little.

"Yes," she cried, hitching her legs around my waist.

"Needy little thing, aren't you?"

"Yes... *yes.*"

Dayna's hands were everywhere. In my hair, under my t-shirt, wrapped around my biceps. It was as if she couldn't get enough, and I loved it. I loved the way she was desperate and needy for me.

I glanced up, scanning the beach. We were secluded, and it was dark down here. No one would know.

No one except me, Dayna, and my conscience. And I'd never really had one of those.

Trailing my hand down her face, I stared at her.

"What?" she asked.

"You sure?"

"Yes."

My fingers dipped into her underwear, finding her center.

"God, please, Aiden." Dayna writhed against my touch as I slowly pressed two fingers into her. Her eyes fluttered as she inhaled a ragged breath.

"Eyes open, freckles. I want to watch you come."

The second she looked at me, I curled my fingers deeper.

"Oh my God." A shiver went through her.

"Feel good?"

"So good. Kiss me. I need you to kiss me." She pulled me down to her, fixing her mouth to mine, moaning against my lips.

Something was happening inside me. A need I'd never felt before. I wanted to own her. Brand and claim her. This wasn't only sex. It was something more.

Something that had the power to fucking ruin me.

Shit.

"Aiden, what is it?" She palmed my cheek. "What's wrong?"

"Nothing." I kissed her, hiding the panic clawing inside my chest as I worked her with my fingers.

"Yes... like that," she cried, arching into my touch. "God, yes."

Her breathing turned ragged as her body began to tremble. I rolled my thumb over her clit, pushing her closer to the edge.

"Come for me, freckles," I whispered, licking into her mouth. "Come for—"

My name on her lips filled the air as she came all over my fingers. Pulling them away, I brought them to my mouth and licked them clean.

Dayna stared at me, all doe-eyed and sated. "That's... wow, that's really hot." Heat flooded her cheeks, and she looked so fucking adorable lying there in the sand.

"I need to get inside you," I grabbed her hand and pushed it to my dick, letting her feel how hard she made me.

"Condom?" she asked.

"Yeah." Pulling my wallet out of my shorts, I pulled out a foil packet and threw it down beside me while I rocked back on my haunches and pushed her skirt up her body. Then I popped the button on my jeans and pushed them down my hips.

"Holy cannoli." She licked her lips at the sight of my length.

"Wait until I'm inside you."

"Hurry."

I made quick work of rolling on the condom and lowered myself back over her. "Last chance to stop this."

Dayna shook her head. "I want this. I want you."

Thank fuck.

Because I needed to be inside her. I needed to feel her tight pussy clenched around me.

Grabbing her thigh, I slowly worked my way inside her, filling her inch by inch.

"Sweet baby Jesus," she moaned, burying her face into the crook of my neck.

"Eyes, freckles. I need to see your eyes."

Dayna laid back down, smiling up at me. She may as well have reached inside my chest and fisted my fucking heart.

What was she doing to me?

"You feel amazing," she said, meeting me thrust for

thrust, our bodies moving in perfect synchrony. It felt good—too fucking good. I already knew one night wouldn't be enough. I wanted to take my time with her. Lay her out on a bed and learn all the ways to make her blush and moan and scream my name.

One night.

Fuck that.

If I had anything to say about it, this was the first night.

First of many.

"Tilt your hips," I rasped, sliding my hands under her ass to lift her onto my dick. Deeper. Harder. I rocked into her. Over and over and over.

"God, that's—" She swallowed a moan, pressing her lips together as our bodies moved together.

"You feel so fucking good." I dropped my mouth to her neck, latching onto the soft skin there and sucking. I wanted to mark her—some primal need to see her skin pink under my touch.

"Aiden, more... I need more."

"You want it harder, freckles?"

She nodded, her eyes alight with desire.

"Your wish is my command." I really gave it to her then. Sand flew up around us as I fucked her in the shadows on the beach. I wasn't really one for getting it on in public, but something about being out here with Dayna drove me wild.

"Aiden... Aiden... ah, God..." She moaned over and over, panting as I drove into her.

"You gonna come for me again, freckles?"

"Yes, yes." She slammed her palm into the sand, locking her legs around my hips as I thrust into her.

Slipping a hand between us, I rubbed her clit to get her there, her pussy tightening around my dick, sending me straight over the edge.

"Fuck..." I groaned. "Fuuuuck." Tingles shot down my spine as I came hard, holding her soft body against mine like it was fucking meant for me.

Dayna nuzzled my chest, kissing a little trail up my throat and over my jaw until she was right there. Breathing my air.

"That was amazing." She beamed at me.

"Give me ten minutes, and we can go again," I chuckled, rolling off her and flopping back into the sand.

"It's late. We should probably think about heading back."

What the fuck?

I glanced over at her and frowned.

"What?" she asked, smoothing down her skirt.

"Are you trying to get rid of me?"

"What? No. I'm just saying we should probably head home."

"Right. Yeah." Dejection sat heavy in my chest as I discarded the condom and clambered to my feet. Thankfully, I found some tissue to ball it up in and shoved it in my pocket until I found a trash can.

Caught up in the moment, things had been scorching hot, but now the temperature had turned colder than Lake Erie when it froze over, and I didn't like it.

"Hey," she grabbed my arm as I went to walk off. "Are you okay? You're acting weird."

"I'm fine."

"Okay, because I don't want things to be weird between us, Aiden. Tonight was— it was amazing. Thank you."

Thank you?

She was thanking me.

I was so fucking confused.

"I'm glad it was you. Now I can move on and..."

I didn't hear past move on.

She'd used me to *move on*.

I was her fucking rebound.

It shouldn't have bothered me, but it did. Because I'd wanted more than one night, and that was a first for me.

"Aiden?" Dayna smiled.

"Uh, yeah. We're good."

"Well then, friend, you can walk me home." She laced her arm through mine as if she didn't have a care in the world.

As if she hadn't just kicked me in the fucking balls.

Friend.

I was pretty sure friends didn't fuck the way we just had, but what did I know about being friends.

Or anything more than that.

The next morning, I was like a bear with a sore head. I'd barely slept. Too wired from the night before. From images of Dayna writhing beneath me, crying for more. For a woman who hadn't had sex in almost four years, her body sure knew what to do.

Fuck.

She'd blown my mind.

The whole night had.

But then she'd acted as if it was nothing. Just two friends getting down and dirty on the beach, doing each other a favor.

I was her rebound.

Jesus Christ.

I'd walked her home, and she'd given me a smile and a wave, reminded me that we should keep things between the two of us, and then skipped into her house as if I hadn't been inside her only minutes earlier.

It didn't sit well with me.

But there wasn't a whole lot I could do about it. She was Carson's friend, and he'd made it more than clear that I needed to stay away from her.

Then there was the little fact that I didn't do relationships. I didn't have the time or energy for something serious. Had no interest in settling down. Not when there was a whole world of pussy out there, especially once I hit the pros.

So why the fuck couldn't I get her out of my head?

I was Aiden fucking Dumfries. I didn't get attached.

Ever.

"Morning." Carson wandered into the kitchen. "Did Dayna get home okay last night?"

"Uh, yeah. Why?"

"No reason." His eyes narrowed. "Why? Did something happen?"

"No." The lie was like ash in my mouth. "Walked her home and then came back here."

"Was she okay?"

"Yeah, I mean, I think so. Why?"

"I'm just worried about her. After Dalton, Dayna fell apart. It was a rough time."

"She'd lost her brother; it's understandable."

"I know." He dragged a hand down his face. "But then she went off to college, and it's like she kept her new life and her life here separate. I don't want that fucker Josh to undo all her progress."

"She seemed fine to me." I shrugged.

"She was ass over elbow drunk, dancing in Moonies."

"And I'm guessing that's not usual Dayna behavior?" A sinking feeling spread through me.

"No, no, it is not." He made himself a mug of coffee and leaned back against the counter. "Dayna's more of a color-inside-the-lines kind of girl. But if you say she got home okay, then maybe I'm worrying for nothing."

Guilt curdled in my stomach. She hadn't been that drunk, had she?

Things were kind of a blur.

"I'm sure she's fine," I mumbled. "I'm going to go for a run."

I had a fuck ton of energy to burn.

CHAPTER 13

DAYNA

I WAS A COWARD.

All that Dutch courage I'd had two nights ago disappeared the second I woke with the headache from hell and an unfamiliar ache deep inside me.

I'd had sex with Aiden.

Sex with Aiden freaking Dumfries.

On the beach, no less, with liquor in my veins and recklessness in my heart. But strangely, I didn't feel any shame or regret for my actions, the way I'd begged him to kiss me, to take me right there in the sand. No, what I felt was something else entirely.

But it was one night—that was all we'd agreed.

So like a coward, I'd hid, feigning a stomach flu. Not that he'd tried to contact me.

He hadn't.

But by the third day, I couldn't fake it any longer because Mom invited Carson and Aiden over for a cookout and insisted that I join them.

"There she is," Carson said as I reluctantly joined them out in the yard. "How are you feeling?"

"Better, thanks." I gave him a tight smile.

"You should lay off the shots for a while."

"Dayna Bug," Mom gasped. "You told me you didn't drink that much."

"I didn't." I shot Carson a hard look, and he chuckled under his breath.

"Don't worry, Judy. Aiden looked after her."

The knot in my stomach tightened at his innocent words, and I couldn't help but glance over at Aiden as he chatted with my dad at the grill.

"Bug?" Carson called.

"Yeah." My smile was forced as I looked back at him.

"You sure you're good?"

"I'm fine. I'm just going to grab a drink. Does anyone want anything?"

"Can you grab the bag of chips off the counter? I think there's some dip in the refrigerator too."

"Sure, Mom."

"Carson, son, get over here," Dad called, and I was relieved Carson wouldn't follow me.

I slipped back into the house, giving myself a second to catch my breath. I hadn't expected things to feel so weird between Aiden and me, but what did I really expect?

We'd had sex.

Sex.

God, no matter how many times I said it, it didn't get any less unbelievable.

I didn't have sex with random guys. I didn't have sex, period. But it'd been so good. So freeing to throw caution to the wind and just let go for once. It helped that Aiden knew what the hell he was doing too.

He'd done me a huge favor. Maybe now I could enjoy dating again. Get back on the horse and make up for lost time.

Who was I kidding?

I didn't want to start hooking up with guys. I'd just wanted to feel *something*. And yeah, maybe a part of me had wanted to get back at Josh for cheating on me.

Anger zipped up my spine; I was so done with his bullshit. He'd been calling and texting me nonstop even though I was ignoring him.

I grabbed the dip from the refrigerator and turned

to get the chips, only to find Aiden standing there, watching me. "Jesus," I cried, my heart lodged in my throat. "You scared me."

"You're avoiding me," he said.

"No, I'm not." I grabbed the chips and made for the door, but he blocked my path, staring down at me.

"I think you are." His eyes narrowed.

"I was sick."

His brow lifted. "If you say so."

"Aiden, can we not—" I went to move around him, but he grabbed my arm.

"Why are you being so weird?" he asked.

"Because... we had... *sex*, Aiden. On the beach, I might add." My cheeks burned at the vivid memory.

"It's just sex, freckles."

"Just sex... right." Unexpected emotion bubbled up inside me.

He was right.

It was just sex.

I'd said that. I'd said it was one night. Yet, hearing him say the words made my heart sink.

God, did I want it to be more?

"Excuse me," I said, yanking my arm free and moving around him. "I need to—"

"Dayna, wait."

But I took off into the yard, unwilling to make a fool of myself any more than I already had.

The whole evening was painful. I barely spoke to anyone, lost in my thoughts. In stupid, foolish thoughts of Aiden and me and the start of something more than *just sex*.

Carson watched me like a hawk, obviously sensing something was wrong. But he didn't ask, and I didn't feel like telling him that I'd had sex on the beach with his star hockey player. Something told me it wouldn't go down too well.

"Are you sure you're okay, sweetheart?" Mom asked. "You've been awfully quiet."

"I'm fine, Mom. Just tired."

"I know breakups can be rough, Dayna, but Josh doesn't deserve your heartache." Disapproval coated her words. "It's obvious the two of you—"

"I'm not upset about Josh."

"So you keep saying, sweetie. But it's never nice being betrayed like that. Even if he wasn't the right guy for you."

"I thought you liked him?"

"I did, but you weren't exactly compatible."

"Mom!"

"I don't mean any offense. I just think you stuck with him because he was a safe bet and the opposite of everything you love."

"I..."

I couldn't really argue with that, so I pressed my lips together, glancing over at the men as they inspected their cards. Dad had challenged them both to a game of poker. From Aiden's rapidly decreasing stack of chips, it was apparent it wasn't his game of choice. But the fact he humored my dad and laughed at his jokes and listened to his stories... well, it did something to me.

Damn him. Why couldn't he be the Aiden Dumfries the sports columns loved to write about? Cold with a short temper and an impenetrable layer of ice around his heart.

It would have made things so much easier.

As if he felt me watching, Aiden glanced up, our gazes clashing. My heart fluttered in my chest as he stared at me, so much left unsaid between us.

At least, that's how it felt.

But what did I know about these things? I'd spent eight months hiding behind a guy I knew I had no real future with.

I was a mess—confused and hurt and frustrated with myself. Almost twenty-two years old. I had my entire life ahead of me, but some days, I still felt so lost.

Aiden smiled. A real, honest to God smile that made my knees go weak. "Hi," he mouthed.

"Hi." I tucked my hair behind my ear, blood pounding between my ears.

"Day— oh."

I glanced at Mom, and she gave me a knowing smile.

"Don't look at me like that, Mom. It's not—"

"It's none of my business, sweetheart. I just want to see you happy." She got up to take some dishes inside, leaving me with my thoughts.

A minute later, she appeared in the door, wearing a grim expression.

"Mom, what is it?"

"You have a visitor."

The men stopped talking, all eyes on me.

"He's here?" A shudder ran down my spine. I don't know how I knew, but I did.

Josh was here, and suddenly, I felt nauseous.

"He wants to talk to you," she said.

Carson shoved out of his seat and came over to me. "Do you want me to get rid of him?"

"I... no, we should probably talk." My gaze slid to Aiden, but his expression was a stone mask, giving nothing away.

With a weary sigh, I got up and made my way inside the house. Mom gave me a sympathetic smile as I passed her but didn't say anything.

I still couldn't believe Josh was here after everything. But I had cut him out after seeing that photo, and I knew that we probably needed to sit down and talk like adults.

My stomach churned as I walked down the hall, my hands trembling. Because Josh wasn't the only one in the wrong here. I was too. Things had gotten so messed up along the way, and I'd had sex with Aiden.

I'd—

"Dayna," Josh's voice gave me little comfort.

"Hey."

"Thank fuck. I've been worried sick."

"Really?" I wrapped my arms around myself, keeping a physical barrier between us. "You sure have a funny way of showing it."

"Can I come in? So we can talk?"

"I don't think that's a good idea. We can talk outside."

"Outside?" His eyes flickered with annoyance. "I drove all this way, and you want to talk outside?"

"It's barely a ninety-minute drive."

"Fine, whatever." He stalked off, and I followed, making a beeline for the swinging bench on the porch. I sat down, but Josh stayed standing. "You didn't return my calls or texts," he said.

"Because I have nothing to say."

"Dayna, that's not fair."

"Fair?" I scoffed, feeling the bitter sting of his betrayal. "You fucked some other girl days after telling me you wanted space."

"I... it was a mistake. I was drunk, and she was—"

"A mistake?" Bitter laughter spilled out of me, but his words still hurt. "Why are you here, Josh?"

"Because I love you." He rushed over to me and sat down beside me, taking my hand in his. It didn't comfort me like it used to. "Because I want us to be together."

"We want different things. I see that now."

"Dayna, come on. We can't just throw away eight months together because—"

"I slept with someone," I blurted out.

"W-what?" He bolted upright, glaring at me.

"It was after we ended things."

"You ended things," he sneered, "not me. I didn't want that."

"You had sex with another woman, Josh. You chose that."

"So you went out and decided to fuck some guy like a whore—"

"You need to watch it," a voice said, and Aiden stepped out from the shadows at the side of the house.

"You," Josh's expression turned murderous, and a ripple went through the air. "It was you."

"Aiden, you should go inside. This doesn't concern—"

"Not going to happen, freckles. He doesn't get to talk to you like that."

"Well, isn't this something." Josh barked out a harsh laugh, glaring between us. "You fucked this piece of shit? Dawson Dumfries' son? Wow, Dayna, talk about scraping the bottom of the barrel."

"Josh," I snapped at the same time as Aiden growled, "I said watch it."

"Or what? What the hell will you do about it? Hit me?" Josh stepped toward Aiden. "I looked you up, asshole. Seems you have a problem with your temper. But go for it. Hit me. Then enjoy your final season sitting on the bench."

"Josh, please." I stood up and put myself between the two of them, Aiden at my back. "This isn't helping."

"The guys told me not to wait for you," he spat. "So many times I could have—"

Crack.

Josh stared at me with horror as he brought a hand to his face. "You hit me."

"You don't get to stand there and put the blame on me for all of this." I dropped my hand. "Our relationship wasn't perfect, Josh. I know that. I know I kept you at a distance, and maybe that wasn't fair to you. But it's my body. I get to decide what I do with it." Tears pricked the corners of my eyes, but I swallowed them down.

"Whatever makes it easier for you to sleep at night." He shook his head in disgust. "The two of you deserve each other."

Aiden moved closer, his hand resting on the small of my back, a silent offer of support.

Josh noticed and scoffed again. "He'll use you, Dayna. He'll get what he wants from you, and then he'll throw you away like you're nothing. But maybe that's what you deserve, maybe that's—"

"Enough." The growl in Aiden's chest reverberated through me, and my eyelids fluttered. "You need to leave, asshole. Before I make you."

"Yeah, yeah. I'm going." Josh cut me with a

scathing look that made me wish the ground would open up and swallow me whole.

He stormed over to his car and ripped the door open, ducking inside. It wasn't until it roared off down the street that I let out a weary sigh.

"You okay?"

Slowly, I turned to face Aiden. "I'm sorry you had to hear that."

"I'm not." My brows furrowed as I gazed up at him. Aiden reached out and brushed his thumb across my jaw.

"Your ex is an asshole."

"So it would seem." I dropped my eyes, but Aiden was right there, gliding his fingers under my jaw and tilting my face back to his.

"You did nothing wrong."

"I'm not sure about that. But I'm relieved I saw his true colors now and not a year down the line."

His hand cupped my face, the air crackling around us. There was a tether between us. One I had never once felt with Josh.

"Aiden, I—"

"Bug? Aiden?" Carson's voice rang out, and we jerked away from each other. But we weren't quick enough.

"What's going on out here?" he asked, narrowing

his eyes at me.

"Aiden heard Josh say some things and came to make sure I was okay." I gave him a reassuring smile, but it didn't dim the suspicion in his eyes.

"Something you two want to tell me?"

"Nothing you need to worry about," Aiden said coolly, turning my blood to ice. I glanced at him, frowning, and he added, "I should probably—"

"Wait." I grabbed his hand. "Actually, there is something."

"Dayna," he murmured.

"No, Aiden. Carson should know."

"Know what?"

"Aiden and I got to talking the other night, and well, I kind of asked him out."

"You asked him out?" Carson's expression grew wary. "Dumfries?"

"Yep."

"And what did Aiden say?" He glared at his star player, and I smothered a laugh.

"I... uh..." Aiden stuttered, and I rolled my eyes.

Men.

"He still hasn't given me an answer. I guess he's worried about what you'll say."

"He should be," Carson murmured.

"Carson Bear Walsh. I know you don't mean that.

I'm a grown-ass woman, and Aiden is his own person. If we want to go out on a date. We damn well will."

"I hate to break it to you, Bug, but Aiden doesn't date." Carson almost looked smug about it, but Aiden's expression was one of sheer confusion. "It's his number one rule."

Maybe I shouldn't have ambushed Aiden like this. But I wanted to prove to him that he wasn't the guy everyone assumed he was. He was a good guy underneath all that ice and anger.

A guy I'd felt safe enough to give myself to.

That meant something.

Even if he tried to fool himself it didn't.

CHAPTER 14

AIDEN

Fuck.

This was a shit show.

I hadn't meant to get in the middle of Dayna and Josh like that, but something inside me snapped when I heard him saying all those things to her.

She deserved better.

Better than you.

My entire life, I'd lived in my father's shadow. Once people learned my surname, they assumed I was like him. That I was a chip off the old block.

I'd hardened to it over the years. Wore it like armor. If it didn't make people weary of me, it intrigued them. But they didn't want to get to know me

—the *real* me. The lost boy underneath years of judgment and hurt.

Dayna looked at me and smiled, and fuck, if she didn't smash her way right through my defenses.

"There's a first time for everything, right?"

I saw the unspoken words in her eyes.

Say yes. Give me a chance.

But I couldn't do it, could I?

I couldn't be the kind of guy she deserved.

I wanted to fuck her again, sure. Wanted it so badly that my dick ached at the thought of getting back inside her. She had felt incredible laid out beneath me on the sand, and I wanted to have her every which way I could. To take my time getting to know her body, her little tells, every way to make her moan my name.

But a date?

Carson was right. I didn't date. I didn't do sleepovers or romance or any of that stuff.

So why did I want it with her?

"I…" Words failed me, and I stood there like a gawking idiot.

Disappointment filled her expression as she pulled away from me, leaving my hand cold. "Well, this is embarrassing." She backed away. "I'm just going to—" Dayna thumbed toward the house and slipped past me without so much as another glance. She ducked inside and closed the door in my face.

Ouch.

"Well, you really fucked that up," Carson said with a mix of amusement and disappointment.

"I... she caught me off guard."

"You're telling me." He scrubbed his jaw. "So when I told you to stay away from her, I'm guessing you took that as a green light to—"

"It just happened."

"Yeah. Happens to me all the time too. My dick just falls into some unassuming girl's pussy."

"Seriously?" My brow lifted. "That's Dayna you're talking about."

And I didn't fucking like it.

"You like her." His eyes narrowed. Cold. Assessing. As if he saw through all of my bullshit.

"It's complicated."

"Well, you'd better uncomplicate it because that woman is special," he said. "She's the best of them, Aiden. This shit with Josh should be all the proof you need that she doesn't give herself to just anyone."

"Shit, you think I don't know that?" I rubbed the back of my neck and blew out a long breath. "I fucked up."

"Yeah, you did, Dumfries. The question is, what are you going to do about it?"

My eyes snapped to his, narrowing. "You're giving me your blessing?"

"Hell no. I'm telling you that if you ever hurt her, you can kiss your senior year with the Lakers good-bye." His words sounded serious, but a faint smirk traced his mouth. "I don't know what's really going on with the two of you, but I also know that you're both old enough to make your own mistakes."

"Geez, thanks for the vote of confidence, *Coach*."

His smirk grew. "Just promise me, you won't knowingly hurt her. That's all I can ask."

"I would never..."

"Yeah, something tells me that's the truth. I'm going to find Derek and see if he'll break out the good stuff. I need a strong drink after this." He walked off, but I called after him.

"Coach?"

"Yeah, Dumfries?"

"Thanks for everything."

He gave me a small nod and disappeared around the side of the house.

I stared at the door, thinking about what he'd said. I didn't know how to fix things, but I needed to at least see Dayna and apologize.

But before I could knock on the door, it swung open.

"Freckles, what are you—"

Dayna threw herself at me, anchoring her arms around my neck. "I'm going to kiss you now," she said. "And I'm really hoping you'll kiss me back."

I smiled against her lips and chuckled.

This girl.

This fucking girl.

"Well, hotshot? What do you say?" she grinned up at me, and I lowered my face to hers, breathing her in.

"Your wish is my command."

"We're going to head in," Mr. Benson said. "It was good seeing you, Aiden. We'll have to do it again soon."

"Sounds good, sir."

"Please, call me Derek, son."

"Son?" Dayna mouthed as she fought a grin.

"Behave," I whispered, my chest tightening at the whole interaction.

"Goodnight, Mom, Dad."

"Night, sweetheart. See you in the morning."

Dayna's parents headed inside leaving me alone

with their daughter. It was strange as fuck, knowing they trusted me out here with her. But I liked it.

I liked them.

They'd welcomed me into their family without hesitation or judgment. And even though I'd told Carson more than once that I didn't want to be adopted by the Bensons for the summer, it felt pretty fucking good that they wanted me around.

"Do you think they know?" Dayna asked, shifting up onto her knees on the patio sectional.

"Know what?"

"That I've thought about nothing but kissing you since we came back out here."

"You have, huh?" I dipped my head, brushing my nose over hers.

Jesus. She was under my skin.

After she'd kissed the shit out of me outside her house, we'd agreed to spend some more time with her parents—without telling them about us—and then talk.

I guess the talking part came now.

Although from the glint in her eyes, Dayna seemed to want to do a whole lot more than talk.

"Is this okay?" she asked, and I frowned. "I don't want to push you into anything you're not ready for. But I meant what I said, Aiden. I like you, and I think there's something here. Something I'd really like to explore. But I know you don't date."

A beat passed while I tried to figure out what to say. Her expression fell, and I cupped her face, bringing her eyes back to me. "I want to try."

"You do?"

"Yeah." Fuck. My heart was fit to burst out of my chest. But she was right—there was something between us—something I wanted to explore further.

I didn't want to hurt her, though.

"But I need to be honest with you, freckles." I touched my head to hers, breathing her in. "I've never done this before."

"You're scared."

"Of hurting you, yes."

"I'm not asking you for anything you don't want to give me, Aiden." She ran her fingers up my chest, her touch igniting a wildfire inside me. "We can take it one date at a time."

"One date at a time, huh?" I smiled against her lips, stealing a chaste kiss.

"What do you say, hotshot? You think you're up for the challenge?"

"I think I'm up to something." Grabbing her hand, I pressed it against my rock-hard dick.

"Aiden!" she gasped, all shock and innocence, but I

saw the heat in her eyes. The hunger.

"You love it, freckles."

"Yeah, I think I do." She curled up into my side, letting out a contented sigh. "Why is it like this?"

"Like what?"

"Like I want to tear your clothes off and—"

"And what?" I whispered against her ear, a bolt of lust shooting through me at the way she shivered.

"Aiden, don't tease me."

"I'm not teasing you, freckles. I want you to use your voice. Ask for what you want. Tell me what you like and what you don't. I'm not going to push you for anything you're not ready for, and I'm not going to ask for more than you're willing to give. But if you want to explore... things with me, I'm down. So fucking down."

She curled her fingers into the hair at the back of my neck and kissed the corner of my mouth. "People are wrong about you, you know. So wrong."

"Only for you, freckles," I said thickly because this wasn't me. I didn't whisper sweet nothings in girls' ears and make them promises.

"Aiden, what's wrong?"

"I just... fuck, Dayna. You've got me all twisted up inside," I confessed.

"Well, I'm not exactly immune to your charm

either." She grinned. "I know you're probably freaking out—"

"I'm not. At least, not in the way you're thinking."

"Look, let's promise each other something."

"I'm listening."

"Honesty." Dayna inhaled a sharp breath. "If you want to stop whatever we're doing, you'll tell me. And I'll do the same."

"That sounds very grown up and mature," I smirked, and she batted my chest.

"Don't mock me."

"I'm joking." I curved my hand around the back of her neck and drew her in for another kiss.

"Aiden, my parents—"

"Aren't fools. Pretty sure your mom was dancing in her seat at all the sultry looks you kept giving me."

"I was not."

"Keep telling yourself that, freckles."

Her expression sobered. "So, we're really doing this?"

"Tomorrow night," I said.

"Tomorrow?"

"Yeah. You, me, and our first date."

"First date?" Her eyes lit up.

I pulled her down to my mouth again and chuckled, "We'll see how it goes, freckles."

CHAPTER 15

DAYNA

"Oh sweetheart, you look lovely," Mom said when I stepped into the kitchen.

"Thanks, Mom."

"Are you excited about your date?"

"Nervous." I sucked in a sharp breath.

I hadn't needed to fess up to her about Aiden, she knew. A mother's intuition, she'd said. Of course, she'd taken the liberty of telling Dad about my budding romance with Aiden. But they were both supportive, and I loved them all the more for it.

"You know, you're more like our Dayna Bug around Aiden. With Josh, you seemed... different."

"I don't think it was just Josh, Mom. It was me," I

admitted. "I was hiding in Boston. I don't want to hide anymore."

"Oh, sweetheart, come here." She came over and pulled me into her arms. "Your father and I are so proud of you, and we love you so, so much. Dalton would want you to live, baby. He would want you to go after all your hopes and dreams and live."

I nodded, smiling over the lump in my throat. "Gosh, I'm a mess, and I need to leave in a minute."

"Here." She went over to the faucet and ran some paper towels under the water. "Give a little dab under your eyes, and you'll be good to go."

"Thanks, Mom."

"A date." She clapped her hands. "It's so exciting."

"Okay, I'm leaving now."

"I want to hear all about it when you get home."

"Sure thing, Mom." I waved her off with a chuckle as I headed out to my car.

Aiden had wanted to borrow Carson's truck and pick me up, but I wanted to avoid my parents making a big thing out of it. I was nervous enough without them peeking out of the windows, watching our every move. Besides, I had organized everything, so really, it was my surprise for him.

The drive to Carson's house was too short. I

needed more time to compose myself, to give myself a pep talk.

Aiden was only the second guy I'd ever gone on a date with. A guy who avoided dating like the plague. But he wanted this.

He wanted me.

I didn't doubt that, not even a little bit. But he was different here. It was the summer. The team and all that came with it were a distant memory. Once he went back to college, though, everything would change. But I was trying hard not to think about that.

As I pulled onto Carson's Street, his truck was nowhere to be seen, thank God. I cut the engine and climbed out, rubbing my clammy palms down my jeans. Despite the balmy heat from the summer sun, I'd dressed for the occasion.

Inhaling a deep breath, I walked up to the door and knocked. It swung open, and Aiden grinned. "You're late."

"I am not."

"Three minutes, freckles."

"I..." My eyes narrowed, and he chuckled, hooking an arm around my waist and pulling me inside. My hands went to his chest, steadying myself.

"Hey," he said, gazing down at me.

"Hey."

"You look..." Aiden's lips grazed my ear, sending a shiver through me. "Good enough to eat."

"While that does sound tempting, we have to go."

"Are you going to tell me where you're taking me, yet?"

"No, it's a surprise." I went to pull away, but he tightened his hold on me. "Aiden, we need—"

"Just one taste." He cupped the nape of my neck right as his lips crashed down on mine. I clung to him, my fingers twisting into the t-shirt stretched against his muscular chest.

"Mmm, that's better." Licking his tongue into my mouth, he teased me, his eyes dancing with heat and humor.

"I... okay, then."

He'd rendered me speechless.

Flushed and breathless, I slipped out of his arms and hurried out to the car, his laughter following me the whole way.

"So, what do you think?" I peeked up at Aiden as he stared out at the rink. "I thought you could show me some of your moves."

"I... hell yes!" He picked me up and swung me around, dipping his head to brush his lips over mine. "This is perfect. I've missed the ice."

"We've got the place to ourselves for ninety minutes."

I'd called in a favor to Ben, the owner. He was a family friend and had been all too willing to let me bring the Lakers star player along for some time on the ice.

"I just need you to sign a hockey jersey for the owner before we leave."

Aiden's eyes crinkled. "Oh, it's like that, huh?"

"Like you don't spend your days at Lakeshore U signing napkins and girls' boobs," I teased, my stomach churning a little at the thought.

We still had a lot to talk about, but I was content living in the moment for now. And it had been too long since I'd been on the ice.

"I'm a little rusty," I said as we got into our skates.

"Don't worry. I'll catch you if you fall." Aiden's eyes twinkled, and I shook my head, laughing at his cheesy attempt at flirting.

"Has anyone ever told you your ego needs its own room?"

"You love my ego." He smiled over at me, a flash of vulnerability in his gaze.

"What's wrong?" I asked.

"I've never... Shit, Dayna," he breathed. "I just wanted to say thank you for arranging this. I figured you'd want to go to some fancy restaurant or something."

"Actually, I thought we could get pizza after this and go sit on the beach." Aiden finished lacing his skates and dropped to his knees in front of me. "What are you—"

"Let me." He gently shoved my hands away and took over lacing my skates, the intimate action sending my heart into a tailspin.

"You know, I haven't been here since..." The unspoken words hung between us.

The rink was one of Dalton's favorite places growing up. I'd tag along with him and Carson to watch them practice. They always had an audience, even back then. But no matter how girls vied for their attention or how many guys hung around wanting to shoot the shit with them, they never left me out.

Laying one of his hands along the side of my neck, he stared at me. "I can't pretend to know what it was like to lose your brother, but he'd want you to live, Dayna."

A ball of emotion lodged in my throat, but I managed a small nod.

"You good?" he asked.

"Yeah, come on."

Aiden helped me up and led me onto the ice. I was like Bambi at first, wobbling all over the place. But he was patient, helping me find my footing before he kissed me and took off like a rocket, zipping across the ice.

"Show off," I called, my voice echoing through the small building. Dupont Beach Ice Rink wasn't much, but it held some of my most treasured memories of Dalton.

Aiden chuckled as he circled me, the grinding of ice filling the frigid air. He was something to behold, cutting across the rink with the grace of a figure skater and the power of a two-hundred-pound hockey player.

I managed to skate to the boards and lean against them to watch him.

"Come on, freckles, get out here," he said.

"I think I'll leave it to the pro."

He came to an abrupt stop in front of me, spraying ice everywhere. His cheeks had the cutest flush, his hair falling in his eyes as he came closer.

Aiden's love of skating was written all over his face.

"Did you always want to be a hockey player?" I asked.

"Come here." Aiden positioned me in front of him,

his arms wrapping around my waist. "Okay?" I nodded, and he added, "Now, gently."

The momentum of his big, sturdy body pushed me forward, and we skated gently around the rink.

"My mom bought me skates for my fifth birthday," he said. "She got them from the thrift store. They were one size too big, so I had to double up on socks. But I was so excited."

"I bet you were the cutest."

"I'm not sure about that." His laughter fanned my cheek. "But I was so fucking stubborn. The lake behind our house used to freeze over in the winter. I spent hours out there, teaching myself to skate. Trying to mimic the moves I saw on television whenever I watched hockey games.

"She worked every second she could to buy me better gear. I joined a local peewee team, and the coach said I was a natural. But I was Dawson Dumfries' kid, too. And people were wary of me, of what it meant to get close to me."

"I'm sorry." I twisted back to look at him, but Aiden captured my lips in a soft kiss.

"Hockey saved me, Dayna. It gave me a purpose, a focus. I was screwed up over my old man, the things I saw and heard about him. Over time, it became this ugly thing inside me. I have a mean temper, and I struggle with authority. But I want to be better. I want to prove to him and myself and everyone else out there that I'm better than him."

"You are," I said.

"And if I'm not?" His words made me push back against him slightly, and we came to a stop. I turned in Aiden's arms, gazing up at him.

"You know the difference between right and wrong, Aiden. You're not here because you stole from someone or hurt someone without good reason. You were standing up for your mom because you love her. Because you protect the people you care about."

"I broke some asshole's nose in the middle of a diner."

Quiet laughter spilled from me. "Okay, so maybe that wasn't the best display of your moral compass, but he was disrespecting your mom. I'm sure he deserved it."

His eyes lit up. "Oh really, it's like that."

"What?" I shrugged, fighting a smile. "It's kind of hot."

"You know what would be really hot?" My brow arched, and Aiden chuckled, dropping his eyes down my body. "You, naked, in nothing but those skates."

"Nice try, Dumfries." I swatted his chest. "But I'll need to get a hell of a lot more comfortable on the ice before I let you talk me into fooling around out here."

"But it's a possibility?" His eyes darkened.

"Aiden!"

"Joke, I'm joking." He hooked an arm around my neck and dropped a kiss on my head. "I didn't think this would be so easy."

"Neither did I."

But he was right; it felt easy.

Almost too easy.

I wasn't going to fret over it, though. Mom was right. He made something light up inside of me, something I thought had long extinguished when Dalton died.

And I wanted to soak it up for as long as possible.

"If the guys could see me now, do you know how much shit they'd give me?" Aiden glanced over at me, and I frowned.

"Let me guess, none of them have girlfriends. Not that I'm suggesting... we're... I mean, I'm not—"

"Freckles?"

"Yeah?"

"It's okay." Amusement twinkled in his eyes. "Connor has a girlfriend. They've been together since last Halloween. But most of the guys are either too busy to date or too interested in sowing their wild oats as much as possible before life gets serious."

I stared out at the lake, trying not to fixate on his words—on the huge elephant in the room. My life was here in Dupont Beach, but Aiden still had a year of college left, and then if everything went the way he hoped, he would turn pro. Life would become one big adventure.

"I thought we agreed, one date at a time."

"I know." I gave him a weak smile. "I had a really nice time tonight."

"Me too." He leaned in closer, capturing my lips in a soft kiss. "I want that second date, Dayna. And maybe a third and fourth. We have all summer."

And then? I wanted to ask, but I swallowed the words.

A lot could happen in a few weeks.

"How come you didn't enter the draft straight out of high school?"

"Because getting my degree was important to me. It's all my mom has ever wanted, and she deserves to have that, you know? She deserves to see me graduate.

Besides, if the hockey thing doesn't work out, I need something to fall back on.

"And the truth is, I wasn't ready back then. I was angry and hotheaded. Still am, sometimes." He nuzzled my cheek, toying with the ends of my hair. "But playing with the Lakers, being with Coach Tucker and the team, it's taught me a lot about myself and the kind of player I want to be."

I gazed at him, his words resonating with something deep inside me. "I wish everyone could see you like this." His brows furrowed, and I added, "Vulnerable and real. There's so much more to you than meets the eye, Aiden. Your mom must be very proud of you."

"She is." He smiled fondly. "And she'd love you. She's been nagging me for years to bring a girl home. Not that I mean—"

"I guess I'm not the only one running away with myself tonight."

Aiden palmed my cheek. "You make it easy, Dayna."

"It's getting late," I said, standing. "We should probably go."

I didn't want to leave, not yet. But I also didn't want to rush into something. Being with Aiden was so easy; it wouldn't take much to fall headfirst for him.

I needed to retain some measure of control over

my emotions. I'd just gotten out of a relationship with Josh. And regardless of everything else, he had hurt me.

We'd hurt each other.

I wasn't looking to make the same mistakes so soon after.

"How about you give me a ride to your house, and then I can walk back to Carson's house?" he suggested.

"Seems kind of counterintuitive, doesn't it?" A small smile played on my lips.

"Not if it means I get to kiss you good night on your doorstep."

Oh my.

My heart fluttered, and I knew then that taking things slow was going to be impossible.

I liked Aiden—really liked him.

I'd opened up and talked to him about things I'd never talked to another person about, not even Josh.

That had to mean something, right?

"What?" he asked, pulling me from my thoughts.

"Nothing. Come on." I stood and offered him my hand. Aiden clambered to his feet and pulled me into his arms.

"I had a lot of fun tonight, Dayna." He stared down at me, quiet and intense. My heart galloped in my chest as the air crackled around us.

"Fuck," he breathed, and my brows pinched. "You do things to me." His words danced over my lips as he kissed me.

I wound my hands around his neck, kissing him back, silently offering him my reply.

You do things to me too.

CHAPTER 16

AIDEN

THE NEXT MORNING, I was the first up. After Dayna had given me a ride to her house, we'd sat in the car for another fifteen minutes, making out like teenagers.

I couldn't get enough of her.

She was so fucking sweet and sexy. I'd left her breathless and flushed on the Benson porch with promises of a second date tonight.

We had the summer, and I intended to make the most of it.

Footsteps in the hall jolted me from the memories of the night before, and Carson appeared, casting a furtive glance in my direction.

"Good morning." I flashed him a wolfish grin.

"Morning," he grunted.

He was pissed, and I got it. I did.

He'd warned me to stay away from Dayna, and I'd broken my promise. But she wasn't like other girls. This wasn't a casual hookup. I liked her—I liked her a lot.

I'd tried to stop myself, but she made it impossible. Because being around Dayna was addictive. And the second I'd had a taste, I knew it would never be enough.

Carson continued to glare at me across the counter.

"Is this the part where you threaten to chop off my balls if I hurt her?" I asked.

"Oh, I won't just chop them off... I'll have the team run shooting drills with them."

A violent shudder ran through me. "I like her, Carson. I really fucking like her."

"Yeah, I know." He ran a hand over his jaw, studying me. "But it's one summer, Aiden. One summer, and then you'll go back to Lakeshore U, and she'll be here, in Dupont Beach. You have hockey, and she has her internship. Doesn't leave much time for a relationship."

"With all due respect, Coach," irritation coated my words, "that's for the two of us to figure out."

I knew he meant well. He wanted to protect me as much as he wanted to protect Dayna. But I'd realized last night that I wanted to give this thing with her a chance.

Dayna was special. She wasn't like the girls at college. She cared about me. She cared about the guy beneath the hockey jersey.

"She's family, Dumfries." A muscle twitched in his jaw. "Fuck her over, and you fuck me over."

Jesus.

His icy glare was enough to send most guys running for the hills. But I wasn't most guys, and I was used to his hard-assed tactics on and off the ice.

"I don't want to jinx it, but I think it could be the start of something."

I hadn't come to Dupont Beach looking for it, but it had found me anyway. And the truth was, Dayna was everything I never knew I needed. Smart, patient, and willing to stand up for what she believed in, and she fucking loved hockey. If anyone could tame my wild heart, it was her.

"Fuck, Dumfries. What the hell am I supposed to say to that?" He chuckled, but his expression quickly sobered. "She's good for you."

"Yeah, she is."

"Just... be careful with her heart. It's fragile. She's

fragile. When Dalton died, it broke something inside her."

"She's stronger than you think."

He gave me a small nod. "So does that mean I can expect to see her around campus a lot on the weekends?"

"You'd have to ask Dayna, Coach." I gave him a small smile. But it didn't sound like a bad idea at all.

In fact, now he'd mentioned it, I couldn't think about anything else. Because I wanted her in the stands, wearing my number, and cheering my name.

"Hopefully, she'll be a good influence because you're on thin ice, Dumfries. One wrong move next semester, and you could jeopardize your shot at the pros before you even step out on the ice."

"You don't have to worry about me, Coach." I planned on turning things around.

"Glad to hear it. So I was thinking we could spend some time together today. Hit the rink and run some drills on the ice?"

"No can do. I have a date."

"Oh, it's like that, huh?" A knowing smile traced his mouth.

"Sure is," I smirked back.

"Well, Dayna better realize you're here to get ready

for next season. That means you have to stick to the workout schedule, Aiden."

"Oh, I'm sure I'll get plenty of workouts, Coach." I couldn't resist.

"No, no fucking way," Carson balked. "That's... she's... Never"—he jabbed a finger in my direction —"talk to me about her like that again, okay? It's too much for my brain to handle."

I got up and walked around the counter, squeezing his shoulder as I went. "Know what I think, Coach?"

"No, but I'm sure you're going to enlighten me."

"You need to get laid."

I walked out of there to the sound of his choked laughter. Carson wasn't a bad guy, and I knew I'd need his support and guidance in the coming months.

And maybe, if things went right with Dayna, I could quit calling him Coach and start calling him a friend instead.

"So, what did Carson say?" Dayna asked as I worked her dress up over her hips.

Much to Carson's amusement, she'd picked me up in her car again for our second date. We'd gone to a little diner on the beach, eating some of the best damn burgers I'd ever had, and then when she'd asked me what I wanted to do next, I'd told her I wanted to go somewhere quiet. Alone.

Dayna had driven us to a secluded spot down by the coast. Just because her parents and Carson knew about us didn't mean I had any immediate plans to fuck her in her bed or my bed at Carson's house.

So car sex it was.

Not that I was complaining. I was desperate to be inside her again. To feel her pussy clamped around me.

"You want to talk about Carson now?" I yanked the neckline of her dress down and started kissing her there. She tasted like salt and vanilla, and I couldn't get enough.

"God, that feels good." Her hands went to my hair, stroking back and forth, sending shivers zipping up and down my spine.

My fingers teased their way down her stomach and between her legs until I found her center, slick and ready. "You're soaked." I hooked her panties to the side and dipped two inside her.

"I want you, Aiden." She ground against my hand, moaning my name.

"I want to watch you come first."

She grabbed my hair and tugged, forcing my eyes to hers. "I want to come with you inside me." Her eyes flared with lust.

"Little Miss Impatient."

"I have a lot of time to make up for," she smirked, tugging at my belt.

"Dayna, let me— fuck," I choked out as her hand worked inside my boxer briefs, fisting my dick and pumping slowly.

"You were saying?"

I gripped the backs of her thighs, dragging her closer. "Put me inside you."

Shit. I froze.

I never went bareback with a girl. Ever. But this was Dayna, and she wasn't any girl.

"We need a condom," I said, desperate to feel her.

"Wait." She grabbed my wrist and gave me a shy smile. "I'm on birth control if you're—"

"I'm clean. And I've never not wrapped it before with other—"

"Aiden?"

"Yeah, freckles?"

"I need you to fuck me now."

Cheeks flushed, lips parted, Dayna rose on her knees a little and tugged my jeans down as far as she could. Enough to grasp the base of my shaft and steady herself as she slowly sank down on me.

"Yes... God, yes."

I buried my face in the crook of her neck, biting the skin there, making her cry out as I bottomed out inside her.

Nothing, nothing would ever feel better than this.

Carson would kick my ass six ways to Sunday if he ever saw us like this. His best friend's little sister and a guy like me. But I was in. I was all fucking in with her.

Sliding my hand up Dayna's spine, I gathered her hair in my fist and pulled gently. "I'm going to fuck you now."

"Good," she panted. "I want it hard and fast."

"Jesus, freckles. Such an innocent face and such a dirty, dirty mouth." I kissed her hard, our tongues tangling together, stroking and teasing.

"Tell me we can do this all summer."

"All summer," I groaned, letting her set the pace. There was nothing better than Dayna taking control and using my body to find her release.

I fucking craved it, like I craved her.

"Promise me." She kissed me, soft and tender, tonguing my mouth the way she rode my dick. Slow and sure, as if she was born to do it.

"I promise."

Dayna stilled, her eyes flashing to mine. A knowing smile tugged at her mouth. "I'll hold you to that."

One date at a time.

That was the deal.

But fuck the deal.

I wanted a summer with this woman.

And who knew, maybe even more.

"Aiden, good to see you, son," Mr. Benson greeted me at the door. "I take it they're not for me." He eyed the bunch of roses in my hand.

"Sorry, sir."

"Maybe next time." He winked, chuckling as he ushered me inside. "We're all out back. Got some prime rib cooking on the grill. I hope you're hungry."

"Always."

"Listen." He stopped and turned to me, forcing me to back up a little. "I just wanted to say thank you."

"Thank you, sir? I... I'm not sure I understand."

"We got our old Dayna back, son. And I'm pretty sure that, in part, we have you to thank for that."

His words knocked the air from my lungs. "I don't know what to say."

"You don't have to say anything, Aiden. Just promise me you'll keep doing whatever you're doing. I haven't seen my Bug happy like this in a long time." He squeezed my shoulder.

There was no way I was telling him that I was almost certain Dayna's new happy-go-lucky outlook on life was down to all the sex she was getting, so I nodded and murmured something about what a great girl she was.

"I'm glad to have met you, son. My Dayna is a lucky girl."

"Not as lucky as me, sir."

"Now, now, I thought we agreed it's Derek."

I nodded, a strange tightness in my chest. I'd been in Dupont Beach less than three weeks, but these people—this family—had accepted me into the fold without question. It was more than I deserved, but I was so fucking grateful.

"You know, Dayna was telling me all about your mom. You should invite her down one weekend. We'd love to meet her."

"I'm sure she'd love that, thank you."

"Anytime, son. Even if you and Dayna Bug hadn't

hit it off, we love having you around. And any friend of Carson's is a friend of ours."

I cleared my throat, trying to dislodge the lump there. "That means a lot, Derek. Thank you."

We headed outside to Dayna and her mom. She got up to greet me while Derek made a beeline for the grill.

"Hey." She smiled, sliding her arms around my waist.

"Hey." I gave her a chaste kiss, aware of Mrs. Benson doing a piss-poor job of not gawking in our direction.

"Is everything okay?" Dayna gazed up at me.

"Everything is perfect."

"Perfect, huh? My dad must have a real way with words." A knowing smirk played on her lips.

"You saw that?"

"I saw the two of you talking. What did he want?"

"That's for me to know, freckles."

She pressed her hand against my chest. "He didn't say anything... inappropriate, did he?"

"He said I should invite my mom down."

"Oh my God," the blood drained from her face, "I'm so sorry. I'll talk to him and tell him that we're—"

"Freckles?"

"Yeah?"

"Take a breath." I smiled. "It's fine. I think it's a good idea."

"You do?" Confusion washed over her.

"Yeah. My mom is dying to meet my girlfriend, and she would love your parents."

"Wait a minute"—her eyes grew wide—"did you just call me your... girlfriend?"

"You caught that, huh?"

Fuck, she looked so adorable, all starry-eyed and flustered.

"So does that mean, if I'm your girl... you're my..." Her breath hitched as if she didn't dare say it.

"Go on," I whispered against the corner of her mouth. "Say it."

"Are you my boyfriend?"

"Yeah, freckles, I think I am."

CHAPTER 17

DAYNA

"Wow, it's great out here," Laura smiled over at me as she tilted her face to the sky, letting the cool spray wash over her.

We were out on The Deke with Carson and Aiden. His mom had arrived yesterday, and Carson had offered to take us out on the boat.

So here we were. My best friend. My boyfriend. And his mom.

But Laura hadn't made any of it weird. She took one look at me when she'd arrived and had pulled me into her arms and whispered how nice it was to finally meet me.

I'd chuckled at that. It had only been a couple of

weeks since Aiden and I had decided to give things a go. But strangely, it felt longer. I guess that's how it was supposed to feel with the right person.

"Yeah, it's nice," I said, glancing over at the guys as Carson instructed Aiden on all things boating.

"He's so different around you." My eyes snapped to Laura's, and she smiled. "Sometimes it takes the right person to bring out the best in us, Dayna. I'm so happy he found you, sweetheart."

There was so much sadness in her voice that my stomach dipped. I knew a lot about what they had endured when Aiden was small, before Dawson Dumfries rose to criminal infamy. But I still didn't know everything.

"Hockey has always been his outlet"—she went on—"his escape, but I always worried that it wouldn't be enough. You can love a sport, but it never loves you back."

"Hockey is his life." I looked over at him again, and Aiden glanced up, flashing me a small, secretive smirk. A bolt of heat went through me.

Damn, I had it bad.

Really bad.

"It is, and I'm so proud of him. But all a mother ever wants for their child is to be loved. To know that another person out there cares the way they do."

Her words settled deep inside me. It was soon, far too soon to be thinking about the future, about what happened after the summer ended. We were both content spending our summer exploring the coast and each other. But I couldn't deny that sometimes my mind did wander. Did think about all the what-ifs and maybes.

I wanted more than one summer, and something told me Aiden did too.

"How are my two favorite girls getting along?" He appeared over my shoulder, his hand curling around my waist as he sat down beside me.

"We're good." I tucked myself closer.

Laura smiled. "This one is a keeper, Aiden. Don't do anything to screw this up."

"Geez, Mom." He let out a thin breath, and we all chuckled.

"I'm just saying. I like her. I like her a lot."

"Yeah." He gazed down at me, sending my pulse soaring. "I like her a lot too."

"Dupont Beach really is a beautiful town," Laura added. "You're very lucky to have grown up in such a wonderful place."

"Yeah, it's the best," I said. "And you're more than welcome to come stay whenever you want. I know my mom and dad are excited you're here."

"That's very kind of them. How are you feeling about your final season?"

"Good. Ready." Aiden shifted slightly. "I've been practicing at the rink almost daily. Ben, the owner, is a big fan. He lets me stay after hours." His fingers tightened on my hip.

I pressed my lips together, trying not to squirm at his unspoken words. Oh, he'd been practicing most nights down at the rink, alright. But it usually ended up with him on his knees, head buried between my thighs, or me bent over one of the benches in the abandoned locker room.

To say we were insatiable was an understatement.

Aiden nuzzled my neck, kissing the skin there, not caring that his mom was sitting across from us with a knowing smile on her face.

"Easy, hotshot," I whispered. "We have company."

"Yeah," he let out a heavy sigh. "I can't wait until we're alone again."

Soft laughter pealed out of me but quickly died when Carson growled across the boat, "What did I tell you, Dumfries? Hands off Bug while we're on the boat."

"Cockblock," Aiden muttered under his breath, and I elbowed him in the ribs.

"He'll come around."

Carson was still sulking, scowling every time Aiden and I got too close, but I knew he was secretly happy for us.

Both of us.

How could he not be? Aiden lit me up inside, and I made him calmer. Softer around the edges. He was like a different guy than the one who arrived in Dupont Beach almost a month ago.

I didn't doubt his old ways would resurface when the semester started, but hopefully, his mom was right. Hopefully, he would realize that it was okay to let the past go.

I had.

And I was more excited about the future than ever.

"More," I panted, rolling my hips in a slow, delicious circle. Aiden gripped my waist, guiding me right where he wanted me.

"You feel so…" *Thrust.* "Fucking…" *Thrust.* "Good." He drove up into me, hitting me so deeply that my eyes rolled.

I leaned down, brushing my lips over his mouth, teasing him with my tongue. But it wasn't enough for him. One of his hands was buried in my hair, his fingers sliding along the side of my neck as he captured my lips in a bruising kiss.

I would never, ever get enough of this. Him. The way he unleashed himself on me. All power and skill. Aiden Dumfries wasn't only the star player for the Lakeshore U Lakers, he was the star of every one of my fantasies come true.

"You going to come for me, freckles? Show me how much you love riding my dick?" He gathered my hair in his fist as I rode him harder... faster, pushing us both toward the precipice.

My hands smoothed over his chest, loving how his taut muscles contracted under my touch. "God, Aiden, it's..." I swallowed, sweat coating my skin.

"Fuck, Dayna, just like that." I clenched around him, grinding down on him. "Fuuuuck," he choked out as an intense wave of pleasure crashed over me.

"Aiden," I cried, everything inside me going tight and loose simultaneously.

"Fuck," he ground out, tensing beneath me as he came hard. "So fucking good." He kissed me, softer this time, and I melted against him, resting my head on his shoulder.

His hands stroked up and down my spine as we lay there.

"This is nice," I said.

"A beautiful girl. Hot as fuck sex. I'm not complaining."

"Hey." I leaned up and gazed down at him. "Is that all I am to you, a warm, willing body?"

I was joking, but something flashed in his eyes. Aiden slid his hand into my hair. "You are so much more than that, Dayna. I hope you know that."

I nodded, too overwhelmed to reply.

"I got you something."

"You did?" A frown pinched my brows.

"Yeah, stay here." He gently rolled me off him and climbed out of bed, not caring that he was butt naked.

"What is it?" I stared hesitantly at the box when he returned.

"Open it and see," Aiden smirked, making my heart flutter in my chest.

I sat up, pulled open the bow, and flipped the lid, my brows pinching at the pale blue tissue paper hiding whatever surprise lay beneath it.

"It won't bite, freckles. But I might later. You look... fuck, babe, you look so tempting like this."

Heat crept into my cheeks. He was always so honest with his words.

"Again? Already?" I teased, knowing full well that he'd probably be ready to go again in ten minutes.

I pushed the tissue paper open, and my eyes went wide. "Is this—"

"Go on," he grinned, "take it out."

The jersey felt soft in my hands as I held it up.

"Figured you'd need your very own Lakers jersey for when you come and watch me play."

"I... I don't know what to say. You bought me a Lakers jersey."

"Not just any jersey." Mischief twinkled in his eyes. "Turn it around, freckles."

No.

My heart crashed into my chest.

No way, he hadn't—

Number nineteen stared back at me.

His number.

"Now everyone will know you're my girl too. I know you're worried about what happens when the summer ends, and I go back to college, but I need you to know that I'm serious about this—us. And I don't want anyone else, Dayna."

"Aiden, I..." I didn't know what to say.

Our relationship was moving at breakneck speed, but it didn't fill me with dread or guilt, or confusion. It only filled me with hope and anticipation, and joy.

"I love it," I said, running my thumbs over the lettering. "Thank you."

"Put it on," Aiden suggested, and I frowned.

"What? I can't. I need to clean up and—"

"Put on the jersey, Dayna. I want to see how good you look wearing my number." His eyes were hooded, simmering with lust as he leaned down, grazing the tip of his nose along my jaw.

"And then I'm going to fuck you in it."

"You have a really beautiful home and life here," Laura said.

It was her final night with us before she returned to Monroe tomorrow. But my parents had already invited her down in a couple of weeks for Dad's birthday celebrations.

"Thank you." Mom smiled. "We've loved getting to know you. And you know how much we love Aiden."

Her gaze flicked to mine and a warm glow went through me. I loved that they loved Aiden so much. It felt so easy being around them all.

"But I'm still number one, right?" Carson joined us, placing down the plate of freshly grilled steaks.

"You know you'll always be number one, son." Dad

clapped him on the shoulder. "But Aiden comes a close second," he added with a smile.

Carson rolled his eyes, taking a seat. "Don't let it go to your head, Dumfries."

"Wouldn't dream of it, Coach." Aiden squeezed my hand under the table.

Some part of him always touching some part of me.

"This looks delicious," Laura said.

"Dig in, please. Nobody is leaving until it's all gone." Mom offered the basket of bread around.

I watched them, my family, my boyfriend, and his mom laughing and joking, and smiled to myself. I felt a peace I hadn't in a long time.

I was home, and I was happy.

And although I wouldn't say the words yet, I was almost one hundred percent sure I was falling in love with Aiden Dumfries.

EPILOGUE

AIDEN

"So this is where you've been hiding," Noah Holden, the Lakers unstoppable right-winger and resident playboy, held out his fist, and I bumped it with my own.

"Holden, good summer?"

"Not as good as yours, apparently." His eyes flashed to Dayna, who was talking to Carson and Austin Hart, our goalie.

"She's a hot little thing," he added around a shit-eating smirk.

"Keep your eyes to your fucking self, Holden," I grumbled.

"Yeah. Yeah. She's yours. Got it." Amusement

danced in his eyes. "Got to say it, man, never thought I'd see the day."

"It's still new."

"Yeah, but you've got that look."

"What look?"

I wasn't sure I wanted to know whatever crap was about to come out of his mouth.

"The 'you'd-give-it-all-up-for-her' look."

"I..." Fuck. He was right.

It had been a month since Josh had shown up on Dayna's doorstep, and made me realize I wanted more than one night from her.

So much fucking more.

We'd spent the month together. Exploring Dupont Beach. Hanging out with Carson on his boat. Having cookouts with Derek and Judy, and even Mom when she came and visited.

Dayna was working at the Erie Echo now, so I didn't get to see her during the week as much. But I often found myself borrowing Carson's truck to drive out to the Echo's HQ and surprise my girl with lunch or a quick make-out session in her office.

The truth was, I couldn't get enough of her. She made me better. She made me dream of things I'd never given so much as a second thought before.

A relationship. A future. Maybe even a family one day.

Yeah, I was in deep.

Deep enough that I expected my teammates to give me shit about it. Especially Holden, the smug fucker.

"Hey," Dayna came over, tucking herself into my side. "You must be Noah Holden."

"And you must be freckles."

"Aiden, you didn't." She glowered at me, and I fought a smile.

"Oh, he did. Hasn't shut up about you in our group chat."

"Holden," I murmured under my breath. Yeah, I was gone for Dayna, but I didn't need her thinking I'd turned into a total pussy.

"Group chat, huh?" Dayna pressed her hand to my stomach, sending a lick of heat through me. I'd had her every which way possible, and it still wasn't enough. But my favorite kind of sex with Dayna was at the rink, every damn time. There was just something about taking my girl at the one place that had always felt like home to me.

"Sounds... interesting."

"So, what do you think of Dumfries' chances of going pro?"

"I think he can do it." She grinned up at me.

"Damn right, he can."

It still felt weird having someone in my corner. Dayna had taken it upon herself these last few weeks to memorize all my stats. And she came down to the rink as much as she could to watch me practice. The fact she used to do it with her brother and Carson and now did it with me was a huge fucking honor.

One I wanted to be worthy of.

"How much are you paying her to say that Dumfries?"

"Oh, he pays me plenty." Dayna's other hand squeezed my ass gently, and Noah barked a laugh.

"Hold on to this one, man. Something tells me she's a keeper."

He wasn't wrong there.

Not by a long shot.

DAYNA

"Hey, Bug. What are you doing in here?" Carson joined me in his kitchen while I watched the party going on outside without me.

"Just catching my breath."

"The guys a bit too much for you?"

"No, everyone's been very sweet."

"Even Holden? That guy is trouble with a capital T."

"Even Noah." I smiled, watching as he, Aiden, and some of the other guys from the team goofed around with a football.

"Penny for your thoughts?" Carson nudged my shoulder with his.

"It's just hard sometimes... knowing that Dalton never got to have this."

"He would have had something to say about you and Dumfries, that's for sure."

"Cars." I rolled my eyes at him.

"What? I'm just saying, if Dalton was around to see you fall in love with a Laker, he would have—" A tear slipped free, and Carson pulled me into his arms. "I miss him too, Bug. But he'd be so proud of you, so fucking proud. Even if you went and fell for a hothead like Aiden."

"You'll watch out for him this season, right? Keep him on the straight and narrow."

"Come on, Bug." His mouth twitched. "You know it's my job to ride his ass."

"Ride whose— Freckles, what's wrong?" Aiden appeared in the doorway.

"Nothing." I wiped my eyes with the back of my sleeve and gave him a weak smile. "I'm fine."

"Coach, do I need to be concerned?"

"Nothing you can't handle, Dumfries." Carson clapped Aiden on the shoulder. "I'll see the two of you out there in a bit." He gave me a kiss on the cheek, and understanding passed between us.

Carson hadn't been happy about Aiden and me at first, but he'd quickly come around. How could he not when I finally felt like I was getting my old self back. The girl who loved her family and Dupont Beach and hockey, and days out on the boat.

I'd stayed away for almost four years when really all I needed was to come home.

And met a bad boy hockey player who pushed me out of my comfort zone as much as he pushed my buttons.

AIDEN

"Freckles?" I pulled Dayna into my arms and gazed down at her.

"I'm fine, I promise. Just silly old grief rearing its ugly head."

"What did I tell you? It isn't silly." Sliding my hand under her jaw, I tilted her face to mine and captured her lips in a soft kiss. "You want to get out of here?"

"No, no. I want to stay. These guys are important to you. And I like Ella. She's really nice."

"Not as important as you are to me," I said. "Ella is good people, though. The two of you can hang out when you come visit me on campus."

Carson had invited the team out to Dupont Beach for a little preseason bonding. It was good to see them. But right now, Dayna is my priority.

She gave me a shy smile. "It'll be nice to have a girlfriend to spend time with."

"I suppose we can hang out with Con and Ella sometimes. When I've gotten my fill of you." I nuzzled her neck, kissing the skin there.

"Aiden, I—"

"Shh." I pressed a finger to her lips, meeting her gaze. "Don't say it, not tonight. Not when I can't immediately bury myself inside you."

Dayna whimpered, "You can't say stuff to me like that when we're in public."

"I can say what I like, freckles. And later, when I've got you all alone, I'm going to strip you naked, lay you out on my bed, and show you exactly what you mean to me."

Because Carson had finally gotten over himself enough to let Dayna stay over.

"You promise?" Her lips curved.

"Oh, I promise." I brought my mouth to her ear. "And if you want to say the words then, I won't stop you."

Her breath caught, and my heart tumbled in my chest.

Because I was gone for this girl.

Ass over elbow in love with her.

The summer wasn't over, but I already wanted more. She warmed me up inside, thawed the ice from around my heart, and I wanted all the summers.

All her firsts.

I wanted a future with Dayna Benson.

And it didn't scare me one single bit.

NOAH

I watched Dumfries and his girl talking and laughing with Connor and Ella. The four of them had hit it off big time. No surprise, given that Con was the only other player on the team with a serious girlfriend. But Ella was good people, and she knew her hockey, so she was practically one of the guys.

"Another one bites the dust," Austin said, coming up beside me.

"You think it'll last?"

"Never known Dumfries to hit the same piece of ass twice, let alone a whole month. It's the real deal."

"Yeah. I was afraid you might say that."

He chuckled, clapping me on the back. "Relax, kid. It means there's less competition." Austin winked and walked off toward them.

But I stayed back.

Aiden and I weren't close. He wasn't really close to anyone on the team. But he was one of the best players we had, and rumor had it, he was going to be captain for the upcoming season. If we were going to make the Frozen Four—and he wanted to catch the eye of a pro team—we needed him to be focused. Not distracted.

Con said something, and Dumfries howled with laughter, gazing down at Dayna as if she hung the fucking moon.

Fuck my life.

It was already happening. She was his world now, and hockey would slowly take a back seat.

"Don't get in between them," a deep voice came from behind me, and I glanced over my shoulder to find Coach Walsh looking at me.

"I would never."

I might have thought about it, but I would never do it. I wasn't a total asshole.

He snorted, "I know that look, Holden. You're worried she'll ruin his season."

"Our season," I corrected. "And from where I'm standing, she looks like a pretty big distraction." Dumfries couldn't keep his eyes off her.

"Dayna is good people, and she's good for him."

"Yeah, I was worried you might say that." I rubbed my jaw, and Coach chuckled.

"Don't worry, Holden. It'll be your turn one day. And I can't wait to see the girl who comes along and knocks you on your ass."

Nervous laughter rumbled in my chest, "Never going to happen."

Coach Walsh gave me a lingering look and smiled. And then he said three little words that had ice sliding down my spine.

"Famous last words."

BONUS EPILOGUE

DAYNA

"Are you nervous?" Ella asked me as we found our seats with our friends Aurora and Harper.

Boyfriend perks meant we were right behind the glass, center rink. The atmosphere in Ellet Arena was electric, five and a half thousand people here to witness the Lakers opening game of the season.

Aiden's final season with the team and his first as captain.

"I can't stop shaking," I confessed, grabbing Ella's hand as we watched the team's congregate on their benches.

I knew what a big deal this was for him, it's all he'd talked about since the summer.

God, it seemed light years ago since I met him on the beach. The grumpy yet cocky guy from Monroe, exiled to Dupont Beach because of his short temper and bad attitude.

We hadn't been together all that long, but it didn't matter. I loved Aiden more than anything. He was my best friend and since we'd recently moved in together, I got to wake up to him every morning, his arm wrapped around my waist, his big, strong body pressed up behind me.

Life was good.

Better than good, life was pretty freaking fantastic.

But I couldn't deny that being here, cheering him and the team on, watching Carson pull Aiden in for a last-minute pep talk, brought a lump to my throat.

"Hey, you good?" Ella squeezed my hand, and I nodded. "He'd be proud of you."

"I know." I inhaled a shuddering breath, feeling Dalton's presence roll through me.

He was gone. But we would always have this.

We would always have hockey.

And now, I got to share my brother's passion with Aiden; to hopefully watch my boyfriend fulfill his dreams.

The referee conferred with Coach Tucker and the coach from the opposing team and then players spilled over the boards, taking up their positions on the ice. Aiden searched the crowd for me, the intensity of his gaze making my heart flutter.

"You've got this," I mouthed, clutching a hand to my chest. He gave me a short, sharp nod and refocused on the game.

The first game of his final season as a Laker.

"Let's go, Lakers," Ella screamed at the top of her lungs, scaring the crap out me. I gawked at her, and she blushed. "Sorry, I get a little carried away."

"A little? I think you burst my eardrum."

"I'm just so excited and nervous for them."

A crackle of anticipation rippled through the arena as the Aiden and the opposing center faced off against each other.

"Come on, babe," I murmured to myself. "You've got this. You've got this."

The referee dropped the puck between them, and Aiden was straight in with his stick.

"Yes," I clapped as he sent the puck flying back to Connor.

"It's going to be a long sixty minutes," Ella grinned up at me.

She wasn't wrong.

But I had a good feeling about things.

I had a good feeling about the season.

"He's all yours." Connor finally emerged from the locker room but there was no sign of Aiden.

I'd been waiting out here forever, wanting to celebrate with Aiden on the team's first win of the season. A shutout thanks to Laker goalie Austin Hart.

"Wait, Con." I grabbed his wrist, and he glanced back at me. "Is everything okay?"

"Go get your guy, Dayna, baby." He winked and took off down the hall.

My heart crashed violently against my chest as I slipped into the locker room. "Aiden?" I called, drawing up short when I turned the corner to find him sitting on the bench, head hung low, negative energy rolling off him in violent waves

He lifted his face, those dark intense eyes of his colliding with mine.

"What's wrong?" I rushed over to him. He pulled me onto his lap, and I wrapped my arms around his neck. "Aiden?" I whispered, stroking the damp hair away from his face.

"I love you, freckles, you know that, right?"

"I love you too." I frowned, my chest tightening. "You're scaring me, Aiden."

"My old man got arrested again." The words landed between us.

"He... he did?"

Aiden nodded. "Mom called. It's bad, freckles. He could be going away for a long time."

"How do you feel about it?"

"Honestly? I don't know." His expression guttered, his gaze darting from mine.

"Hey, hey, look at me." I gently grabbed his jaw and coaxed him back to me. "It's okay to have mixed feelings. He's still your dad. Whatever you need, Aiden, I'm here for you. I'll always be here."

His hand slid up my spine, his fingers curving around the back of my neck. "You, freckles. I only need you." Touching his head to mine, he pulled me closer, our breaths mingling as we stared at one another.

"I love you, Aiden."

"I love you too." His voice cracked. "So fucking much."

A charged beat passed.

And another.

Then we crashed together, all tongue and teeth and utter desperation. Aiden grabbed and clawed at my leggings, and I lifted my ass a little to help him peel them down my body.

"I need to be inside you, freckles. Now."

"I'm right here." I rocked against him, scraping my fingers over his jaw as we kissed and kissed and kissed some more.

Aiden curled his arm around my waist, lifting me off his lap so he could work his pants open. "Hook your underwear to the side," he commanded, his voice thick with desire.

I obeyed, anchoring my hand around his neck as I used my knees to steady myself. Aiden gripped my hip, guiding me over his erection, teasing me.

"Oh god," I cried as the tip nudged my clit.

"Put me inside you," he rasped, his eyes locked on mine.

Shifting a little, I sank down an inch, our mingled groans filling the locker room.

"Fuck," he gritted out, his jaw clenched.

"You feel so good." I lowered my hips, taking him slowly into my body, squeezing his dick as he filled me.

But Aiden couldn't wait, thrusting up and bottoming out inside me.

I cried his name, pleasure sparking inside me.

"Ride me, freckles. Fucking worship my cock." He

leaned back against the wall, hands loosely on my hips as I started rocking my hips, back and forth, side to side. Moving in a figure of eight pattern that I knew drove him wild.

"Fuck yes." One of his hands left my hip to dip under my jersey and long-sleeved shirt. He found my breast, massaging it as I rode him.

"God, Aiden," I moaned, picking up the pace. Rising off him and dropping back down with vigor.

"Mouth, freckles. Give me your mouth."

Our kiss wasn't tender or soft, it was hard and bruising and left my lips swollen and sore. And I loved it. I loved the way he needed me. I loved being the only girl on the planet who got to give Aiden Dumfries what he needed.

"More," I cried, bouncing on his dick, barely able to keep my rhythm. He felt that damn good.

Aiden, sensing my impending orgasm, grabbed my hips and took control, fucking into me like a man possessed.

"Yes, yes... god, Aiden... *god.*" My breath caught, lodged in my throat.

"You look so fucking good riding my dick. But you'll look even better coming all over it." Shoving a hand between us he pinched my clit and I shattered, crying his name over and over as a wave of pure bliss crashed over me.

"Fuck, yes. I can feel your pussy squeezing me, freckles. I'm so," *thrust*, "fucking," *thrust*, "close."

Aiden came with a roar, the sound echoing off the walls, reverberating inside me. I wrapped myself around him, peppering kisses all over his face as he rode out his own orgasm.

"I love you, Aiden Dumfries. More than anything in the world."

"You're mine, Dayna." He dropped his head to mine, searing me with an intense look. "Now. Tomorrow. Always."

Too choked up to reply, I nodded.

Because I didn't just love this man. I wanted a life with him. A future.

I wanted a happily-ever-after.

Forever.

AIDEN

"Where the fuck did you get to?" Noah asked as I leaned up the bar beside him.

"I needed a minute."

"I bet you did." He smirked, following my line of

sight to where Dayna had joined the other girls. "Beer?"

"Thanks." I accepted the drink, taking a long pull. "My old man got arrested tonight," I murmured.

It would hit local news eventually, so it wasn't some big secret. But I still felt a lick of shame saying the words.

"Shit, man. I'm sorry."

"Don't be. It's the least he deserves. You played a good game tonight."

"Thanks." Noah let out a small sigh. "It felt good to be back out there."

"No feeling like it."

"Damn right."

We clinked our bottles together and watched the rest of the team celebrate our first win of the season.

First of many if things went to plan.

When I glanced over at him, I noticed his gaze fixated on a certain girl who had just arrived. "Want to talk about it?"

"Nope." He drained his beer and slammed it on the bar. "I'm going to head out."

"You should stay. Celebrate."

"I can't be here. But have another drink or three for me." Noah clapped me on the shoulder, before disappearing into the crowd.

"Noah left already?" Dayna approached me.

"Yeah. He's hurting."

"They both are." She wrapped her arms around my waist and gazed up at me. "I love you."

"I love you too." I dropped a kiss on her head. "Want to get out of here?"

"Later." She chuckled. "We have to celebrate your first win as captain."

"I can think of a few ways I'd like to celebrate."

"You already at me at the arena. Isn't that enough for now?" Lust shone in her eyes, making my heart flip in my chest.

"No amount of time will ever be enough with you, freckles."

"Okay, Dayna, baby. Put Dumfries down," Connor called as he and some of the other guys stalked toward us. "We need a little one on one time with our captain."

"Guys, come on—"

"Oh, hell no, Dumfries. It's time to celebrate. Laker style."

Dayna stepped away, amusement dancing in her eyes. "Better to go with it," she said. "It'll be easier."

"Thanks for the support, freckles." I glowered as they manhandled me into the middle of the huddle and led me toward the rest of the team.

"Is this really necessary?" I protested.

I loved my team. Loved them all like brothers. But I also loved my girl, and I wanted nothing more than to take her home and bury myself deep inside her for the rest of the night.

"Fuck yeah, it is," Austin bellowed. "It's the first win of the season. We need to celebrate that shit." He thrust a drink at me as they started chanting, "Dumfries. Dumfries. Dumfries."

My name rose like a battle cry shove the background music. Until the entire bar was chanting. Even Dayna mouthed my name, smiling at me with adoring eyes.

"Okay, okay. Here's to our first win of the season," I said, lifting my drink in the air. "The first one of many. Lakers on three. One. Two. Three."

"Lakers!"

Cheers exploded around me as I threw back my drink, wincing at the bitter taste of whatever shit they'd spiked it with.

"If that's the best you can do, Cap," one of the rookies said. "I fear for our season."

"Watch your fucking tongue, Cutler. And remember the golden rule. Five drinks max. I want to see your ugly ass on the ice bright and early."

We'd won one game. We had at least thirty-three

games to go. More if we made it past the regular season.

"Dayna, baby. Get over here and help your guy relax," Connor shouted.

"Trust me, Morgan. You don't want to see Dumfries and his girl relax." Cutler snorted.

"You little shit. Say that again and I'll—"

"Let's go, hotshot." Dayna grabbed my hand and pulled me away from the crowd.

"We're leaving?" My eyes lit up.

"No." She grinned over her shoulder. "We're dancing."

Dayna spun around and pressed herself up against me, swaying her hips in some sexy little move.

"Freckles," I warned, heat curling in my stomach.

Fuck, I loved this woman.

"Dance with me." She pouted. "You know you want to."

Wrapping my arm around her waist, I pulled her closer, burying my face in her neck. "Are you trying to drive me wild?"

"Is it working?"

"Yes."

She chuckled. "I just want you to relax. Enjoy yourself. I know the news about your dad—"

"It doesn't matter," I said, touching my head to hers. "I have all I'll ever need right here."

"You do?"

"I do, freckles. You and my mom and this team. You're my family. My life. My heart."

"Aiden..." Her expression softened, love shining in her eyes.

"I love you, freckles," I said, and I was hit with the clearest mental image of her in a white dress, walking toward me down a flower-lined aisle.

It should have scared the shit out of me.

But it didn't.

Because I wanted that. I wanted a life with her.

A future.

Forever.

PLAYLIST

Summertime Sadness – Lana Del Ray

I Knew You Were Trouble – Taylor Swift

Alive – Sia

Colors – Halsey

Scar – Foxes

Moments – Tove Lo

Perfectly Wrong – Shawn Mendes

Make You Stay – The Girl and the Dreamcatcher

Second Chances – Imagine Dragons

Written in the Stars – The Girl and the Dreamcatcher

ACKNOWLEDGMENTS

Sports romance has always felt like home to me but I wanted to try my hand at a new sport ... and hockey it was! I hope you enjoyed Dayna and Aiden's story as much as I enjoyed writing it. I am SO hyped for this new world, and can't wait to write some more Lakers.

Fifty-something books in and it never gets any easier, but fortunately, I have a great team around me. Huge thanks to my beta team (and resident hockey experts) Jen, Amanda, Carrie, and Jenn. My editor Kate for working around my tight deadlines. To my proofreaders Darlene and Athena for always fitting me in last minute, and my Promo and ARC Team members for being on hand to read and review early copies as well as spread the word. And a special shoutout to my audio producer Kim over at Audibly Addicted for bringing this series to life. You're all amazing!

And finally, to every reader, blogger, bookstagrammer, and booktokker who has read, reviewed, shared, or shouted out about this story – thank YOU! Your continued support makes it all worthwhile.

Until next time...

L A xo

ABOUT THE AUTHOR

Reckless Love. Wild Hearts.

USA Today and *Wall Street Journal* bestselling author of over forty mature young adult and new adult novels, L. A. is happiest writing the kind of books she loves to read: addictive stories full of teenage angst, tension, twists, and turns.

Home is a small town in the middle of England where she currently juggles being a full-time writer with being a mother/referee to two little people. In her spare time (and when she's not camped out in front of the laptop), you'll most likely find L. A. immersed in a book, escaping the chaos that is life.

L. A. loves connecting with readers.
The best places to find her are:
www.lacotton.com